TALES OF TWO CITIES

For Lynn, with so many thanks for her supportive help,

TALES OF TWO CITIES

A NOVELLA PLUS STORIES

Serge

GEORGE FETHERLING

SUB WAY

VANCOUVER

Copyright © 2006 by George Fetherling

Library and Archives Canada Cataloguing in Publication

Fetherling, George
Tales of two cities: a novella plus stories/George Fetherling.

ISBN 0-9736675-1-6

I. Title.

PS8561.E834T34 2005 C813'.54 C2005-906198-7

Subway Books Ltd.
1819 Pendrell Street, Unit 203
Vancouver, BC V6G 1T3 Canada
Website: *www.subwaybooks.com*
E-mail: *subway@interlog.com*

Design and production: Jen Hamilton
Cover photo: Lincoln Clarkes (*www.lincolnclarkes.com*)

Canadian orders:
Customer Order Department
University of Toronto Press Distribution
5201 Dufferin Street
Toronto, Ontario M3H 5T8

US orders:
University of Toronto Press Distribution
2250 Military Road
Tonawanda, New York 14150
Tel: (716) 693-2768
Fax: (716) 692-7479

Toll-free ordering from Canada or the US:
Tel: 1-800-565-9523
Fax: 1-800-221-9985
Email: *utpbooks@utpress.utoronto.ca*

CONTENTS

Some of this book has appeared in different form in
The Fiddlehead, *Geist* and *Paragraph* and in the anthology
Pure Fiction edited by Geoff Hancock.

A TALE OF TWO CITIES

I

Six months after the affair started, Cynthia and I were lying in bed together, both of us totally spent in the aftermath and feeling understandably close. Transported by the intimacy and shared privacy of the moment, I asked whether I could put a question to her.

"Sure."

"What did you feel like after the first time we made love? In that hotel." I was surprised at how soft and low my voice was.

"Angry," she said with no hesitation. I was dumbstruck as usual that she would have been angry (as usual). "I was furious with myself for just climbing into bed that way."

"It wasn't something I did, was it?"

"It was your idea."

Cynthia had this way of ruining moments by talking before she had reviewed her menu of options. Everything went sliding straight from the brainpan and out of her mouth without the smallest consideration of how the words might sound or what effect they would have. In this respect, she was the least Chinese person I have ever known. There is no other way to describe her.

My own recollection of that first time is somewhat different. Cynthia, I realised at once, was the most sexually adept woman I had ever been with, except in one startling particular: she didn't know how to kiss. She simply jammed her enormous tongue down my throat and left it there. No lips against her lover's lips, no quick ins and outs in the dark as snakes use their tongues to feel their way along in the open air. It was more like tongue rape except that she wanted the same thing back. She expected me to force her tongue out of my mouth and stuff mine violently into hers. When I didn't, she got angry. When she called attention to my inexperience, I didn't have the heart to tell her that this was not the way the world kissed, that somehow when she was thirteen or so, back in 1976 or thereabouts, someone simply misinformed her about how the act was carried out. A lifetime's worth of watching movies in which people kiss correctly and passionately had not caused her to doubt herself for a second. I envied that self-confidence even as I found it puzzling and sometimes annoying. But then I was, I admit it, terribly excited by her body. She was one of those people whose white skin had the faintest orange tint that made her seem supremely healthy all the time. Later, after the relationship was over, it reminded me of the trace of colour left in the dishwasher when you forget to pre-rinse a bowl that once contained spaghetti sauce. It is a colour you can never get rid of after that.

We were crazy about each other from the start. I found her style refreshing and mistook her awkwardness for candour. "I haven't seen clothes like that since the Monkees," she said when I turned up for one of our meetings in a bright blue shirt. My natural reticence about hurting her feelings prevented me from pointing out that this was an odd comment from someone who at that moment (though not for too many minutes longer) was wearing plaid woollen trousers, garish and skin tight. This was at least a couple of years before I even knew the term *camel-toes*.

Whenever she said she was angry she was usually only stating the obvious. The first time she announced her anger this way, however, it sounded more like surprise. By this I mean she sounded surprised by the timing, not amazed at the development, as though she had been expecting it for days, like her period.

"I'm so fucking angry," she said, putting a great deal of space round each word and seething with hostility towards, not just me, but both of us. "I swore that I'd never get involved in another long-distance relationship." Later, she spoke often of the LDR, an abbreviation that was new to me at the time.

The affair lasted a year. At the start, it was much more exhilarating for being so long distance. We spent as much as two hours on the phone each night, talking about everything and nothing, the way people do. She was the practical one and signed up for a Sprint long-distance savings package and insisted I do the same. I thought I was completely candid about myself and believed also that I was learning everything about her. Her mother had died when she was only fifty, died on the operating table during what was supposed to be a simple operation to remove an ulcer. She said: "One in every five thousand or so times, somebody who can't possibly survive, does, and somebody else who isn't in any danger dies for no reason at all. I was the number five thousand." She meant that her mother had been. "God, was I angry." She had a younger brother who was ill. Their father, though healthy, was getting to an age where medical matters would be a concern. Most revealing of all, Cynthia herself had suffered some serious, strange and debilitating illness that had kept her in St Paul's Hospital for months. Like money and emotions, this was a taboo subject with her, and I got only little pieces of the story over time. It was some degenerative disease such as MS, but she had beaten it through outrage and resolve. I suppose this reinforced her beliefs about the utility of anger, but I don't want to engage in cheap amateur psychology after the fact.

She was an assiduous accumulator of frequent-flyer points, going far out of her way to hire cars, for example, during times when doing so was what she called a multiplier. So we agreed that she would visit me in Toronto one month and I would visit her in Vancouver the next. In between, we would talk on the phone each day. This was after I suggested that the real strain in an LDR was not necessarily the commuting (personally, I looked forward to the travel) but rather that the two people didn't share the dreary minutiae of their lives over the breakfast or dinner table. "We have the sexy stuff," I said. "What we need to maintain this relationship is the boring stuff as well." She bristled a bit at the word *relationship* (maybe that's why she preferred the abbreviation) but agreed with what I was saying. We also exchanged little notes and even postcards, whether we had spoken on the phone that day or not.

Dear C: Rain here all day, turning to flurries. Thinking of you as I do the kitchen washing-up. Back to the doctor's for more lab tests. Private fears awakened, but then hypochondria has always been my most serious health problem. Up late reading Simone Weil. Do you know her work? Jewish mystic tradition. Converted to Xtianity with a vengeance. Stranded in Casablanca during the war. "Only Christ and Charlie Chaplin have understood the working man." Mystics have always attracted me, but not mysticism. Missing you already and three weeks still to go.

Which is about as many words as I could get on a postcard. Her postcards back were physically more attractive. I believe she must have bought them at the VAG shop near her office, and certainly her handwriting was more appealing than my own, which isn't writing at all but rather drawing, crude and deliberate. She signalled love with little x's and o's at the bottom. At first I thought there might be significance in how the number of x's and o's varied from one card to the next, such as the fact that sometimes she was fonder of me than others or that extra kisses and hugs were supposed to be making up for the days she missed writing. Then I decided no, there was no hidden meaning. The obvious meanings were enough.

As she had business in Toronto, she visited me first. I met her at the airport of course. The first thing she said on entering the house was "Well, *this* is certainly in better taste than I expected." Realising finally how that must have sounded, she clarified the remark. "You must have had help on this," she said admiringly. I just laughed. When I went to stay with her the following month I learned that she lived in what West Coast people call a basement suite. This particular example was not exactly what the English mean by a garden flat. It was a basement surely but there was nothing suite-like about it. The furnace was in the middle of the low-ceilinged living room, hidden by thin Gyproc walls that made a large stubby pillar that blocked the view from one room to the next. She lived this way to save money. She was clearly a dedicated saver. Judging by her place, I surmised that she spent mostly on clothes and CDs. One entire wall of the bedroom was a mirrored closet that held her wardrobe like a bookshelf with too many books crammed onto it. Otherwise the place was neat, orderly and a little spartan: certainly the cleanest semi-subterranean apartment I had ever seen, even if there was a little too much furniture too close together. She decorated with posters that were of course overly large for the wall space but they were custom-framed. She seemed to have some phobia about keeping too much food in the place. Just fresh vegetables and a few cans of tuna at any one time. The lavatory was full of herbal remedies such as echinacea, which like most other people in Toronto I had never heard of at the time but which soon became a commonplace for the common cold; Cynthia would gobble the stuff by the handful. There was also a big plastic bottle of a soft yellow liquid. This was the vanilla extract that was the only cosmetic she used. She always smelled of it at remotely sexual range: a lovely fragrance that will always remind me of her. "I have issues with supporting the pharmaceutical industry," she said.

This was in Kitsilano, former seat of flower power, now the den of decaffeinated professional ambition, a splendid place on a warm clear day when a few of its older but still heliotropic residents emerge with their heads full of memories of the sixties. We would see them strolling West Fourth, where there was a bookstore specialising in both New Age titles and ones about business, or along Jericho Beach. At night we would frequently find something to do together downtown, where with the coming of darkness the city took on a harsh nocturnal glow that was almost metallic. When I look back now on how I first got to know Vancouver, I think of Cynthia of course but also of ads such as "E. Indian Live Phone Sex!! Speaks: Punjabi Hindi Urdu Tamil, $15/call" and the very concept of all-you-can-eat sushi, an idea in which Cynthia found nothing strange whatsoever, not even the rather authoritarian reality of such places. Yes, for one fixed price you could order sushi until you died there at the table but if you ordered something you didn't finish you'd be charged for it at the à la carte price. (And you must go to bed early, without television, and do extra chores as punishment.) It is through food that we first get to know foreign cultures. This is as much true of the West Coast as it is of China or Thailand.

✳ ✳ ✳

What do you want for your birthday? I asked.

A divorce, she said.

Having half my life cut away made the remaining part more complicated. I was living in a vacant house (it was vacant even when I was there) with important papers all over the floor: manuscripts still not read, contracts yet to be negotiated. Finally I got myself together to go to Office Depot and buy five very cheap plastic brief-cases, all bright yellow. I stencilled a different keyword on each one—DIVORCE, WORK etc. One said just T (for THERAPY). I kept them all in a neat row by the door. I thought this was the perfect system but of course it got screwed up. I was having a meeting with the most important publisher in town. I reached down under the boardroom table for my presentation and saw the word DIVORCE two inches high. Later, in the underground garage, I actually cried a little bit. Then I got angry with myself for not colour-coding the fucking things.

It got to the point where I was seeing two different shrinks because I couldn't trust a single individual with everything that was going on. After each session, I would have to hurry to the gents' and scribble down notes on what I'd said, so I wouldn't get confused and pick up the story I'd been telling Doctor A when I was having a session with Doctor B. Therapy was actually making me schizoid, I thought. Eventually I revised my system. Two briefcases, T1 and T2. That made me a better, more organised person. I felt I was on my way to becoming more fully integrated, as Doctor A liked to say.

Doctor A came recommended by everyone I knew, including all my nuttier clients. That was the problem. He is Toronto's pre-eminent literary psychiatrist, specialising in disorders of the creative personality. I think I read once that the Writers' Union made him an honorary life member. The trouble was I kept meeting all these people in the waiting room who were trying to sell me on something or wanted me to sell something on their behalf or whom I owed money to perhaps. As we waited there, they would tell *me* their troubles, as though I were the doctor. One of these hacks sidled up to me once to confess that he was looking for a new agent. "My old one found religion. Jesus appeared to her in a vision. He said He was coming back and wanted her to handle the publicity." Another was always complaining about his ex-wife. "She was only a lesbian long enough to get in all the anthologies."

I couldn't wait for this log-jam of broken souls to clear up so that I could get my turn inside and hear Doctor A say, "So, tell me about your dreams." He wasn't a Freudian of course, but he asked the question like a psychiatrist in a 1950s novel because I told him I liked talking about my dreams, found it helpful. Shows how old-fashioned I am. For this occasion I had memorised two dreams that he hadn't heard yet, though Doctor B (who would sometimes play along but less willingly) already knew them. In the first, a spiv approaches me while I'm waiting for a subway with my yellow briefcases.

"My name is Biscuit," he says.

For some reason, I answer, "I once killed a man named Biscuit. No relation, I suppose."

"I am the one you murdered," he says, and then he pushes me into the path of the train.

In the other dream, there is this old cop ("I'm not the janitor but the next step up") sitting on one of the stools at a diner. There are two loos. One door is marked WOMEN, the other POLICE.

But he didn't want to hear about my dreams. Instead we did a whole session on my distant ancestry. I told him the story of how, when the revolution started in 1956, Grandmother sent her man to the pawnshop with her jewellery, but not the really good stuff. That was the family story anyway. Most of the time the doctor did all the talking. On occasion my attention wandered. More than once I found myself thinking about office equipment. Back in the days when everyone was interested in telepathy, I bought my first fax machine. When I decided I wanted to be cremated, I started debating whether to get a paper shredder.

I should have got one sooner.

✳ ✳ ✳

Every year I would ask Faye to come to Frankfurt with me. It's not so boring as it sounds, I would say; after the book fair, we'll go to Paris on the train. Other years I substituted London for Paris as part of the offer. Once I braced myself and offered to help her get in touch with her ancestral roots in the Scottish Highlands, with its grey rocks and silent angry Protestants as far as the eye can see, dotting the hillsides like sheep. But she never wanted to travel with me at all. At first I assumed this was because she simply didn't like travelling, though she had backpacked in her student days long before we met. Later I decided that she simply didn't like my business, working with authors and publishers. She read, but I never knew how she reacted to what she read. I had not quite figured out that it wasn't travel itself that she didn't care for.

I had no qualms about going to Frankfurt alone again. Father disapproved of course but then he always did. "Whenever I hear the German language, no matter what they're saying, in my ears it sounds like 'Gather your possessions and come with me.'" Business wasn't very good. It never is. People go to Frankfurt not to buy or sell but to schmooze, and you can't put a price on successful schmoozing, which cannot be carried on the books as an asset but of course is one, an important one. I did London on the way back, but not too successfully, because most of my London contacts, built up over the years, a drink here, a breakfast coffee there, were themselves delaying returning to their offices, just as I was doing. Then my traveller's luck deserted me. The details would be boring to relate. Suffice it to say that I spent most of the night sleeping in a chair at Heathrow, as all the nearby hotels had turned on me as well. I was tired and bedraggled, certain I was now too old for such nonsense, when I finally reached Toronto, still in sleep deficit. It was dark. When I opened the door and turned on the light switch, I knew in an instant that Faye wasn't there. I wandered from room to room. In the bedroom the atmosphere was museum-y, and when I opened the closet I saw all those empty wire hangers like executioners' nooses. That's when the phone rang. It was Faye, with what I thought was theatrical—I could almost say melodramatic—timing. As I learned later, she was watching from her car, cell in hand, waiting for me to go through the house, turning on the lights in different rooms. She said she would be staying with a friend from now on and would see me in a few days' time. Her tone was sharp, jagged in fact, angry, almost at a seething boil. I presumed the friend was Gunnar, the stupidly muscular young man who claimed to have been everything at one time or another, from yoga instructor to army commando to financial genius. I was so tired that I seemed to have lost all my peripheral vision. The various sectors of my body felt as though they were joined by piano wire rather than bones and muscle; that I had no more skeletal strength than a marionette. I did the only two things an intelligent person could do in the circumstances. I had a double scotch and went to bed.

※ ※ ※

Everyone knew about Faye and the thick-necked Gunnar. There had even been a snide comment about them in *Frank*, which Faye was too embarrassed, and I too polite, to mention, planted no doubt by some malicious writer: a client who felt he had been wronged or somebody who wished to be a client. (In retrospect, I have come to suspect the young comer Robert Mulligan, author of *The Garburator*, a novel everyone felt had to be read but no one enjoyed or even admired.) What no one could quite figure out was what Gunnar saw in her. He was not only younger than I was, he was younger than she was (and yet had crammed so much imaginary living into so few all-too-real years). I became aware that their relationship was becoming heated after she and I stopped having sex together, for I have learned that death of one sort or another can often be the first warning sign of decay. Originally I couldn't determine whether she simply had gone off me or had climbed on top of someone else. I thought hopefully that the affair (I've never quite grown accustomed to spelling it that way rather than *affaire*) would run its course like the fever I supposed it was. Then I continued to think this but not hopefully. I discovered that I was growing ambivalent about the marriage, both wishing it would end yet afraid of being without it, not knowing how to control how I felt, not knowing what she herself felt. It was at precisely this point that I met Cynthia in Vancouver where I had gone, as I do every year, to teach at the SFU summer publishing workshop. I was vulnerable and she was adventurous. Does that sound as though I'm attempting to obscure or even erase blame? Actually each of us was a bit of both but the proportions were reversed. I was teaching the relationship between author and publisher and the relationship of agent to both. Cynthia was teaching publicity. She asked if she could sit in on my lecture. She sat in and I couldn't take my eyes off her. In my fantasy I could see her oozing out of her clothes and thought that she could read my mind. A man is always flattered when a woman more than ten years younger seems to be interested in him; the laws of probability suddenly evaporate. He is also curious, puzzled and stupefied. Only then does the uncertainty set in, turning to suspicion that cross-fades into terror. I have never been able to determine to what extent the two most important women in my life, Faye and Cynthia, harboured emotions equivalent to mine or to what extent this lack of comprehension on my part was bound up somehow with their being WASPs and I not. These are complicated questions to which I have no answers after so many months and years of searching. I must be content with simply getting on with the story.

Every psychiatrist, even mine, not to mention every television comedian, knows that Jews are born without the ability to metabolise guilt feelings. When it comes to guilt, we are emotional diabetics, producing guilt voluminously in ourselves and others but lacking the insulin to render it harmless. Thus I was practically in traction with guilt over my extreme flirtation with Cynthia even while I was being cuckolded (a word I would have thought had disappeared from the language until I became interested in the internet). Knowing this would be the case, Faye apparently tried to drive me into an even worse state by odd deceptions and mind-games. At least once that I became aware of she was apparently having me followed—and not very professionally if I became aware of it, suggesting to me that I was intended to notice. One day I went to our safety deposit box at the bank to put my passport back in safe keeping, having had it lying round on the dresser since getting back from Europe. I discovered that the box had been emptied. Everything was gone, even the private but harmless papers in a small manila envelope on which I had written TO BE DESTROYED IN THE EVENT OF MY DEATH, a habit I had learned from my father who always did this whenever he went anywhere. I also discovered that a couple of seldom consulted files had disappeared from my home-office. At first of course I assumed they had been mislaid. Perhaps Pam, who helped out there three days a week, had put them somewhere. But she said no. I grew anxious but said nothing to Faye who, doubtless frustrated with my apparent inability to notice her crime, finally blurted it out during one of the increasingly strained but necessary conversations that people who are separated must have. The way she confirmed my suspicion somehow found expression as shock in my voice, to which she replied with lines that only sound stilted on the page. "Yes, I was a real bitch," she said (or snarled or hissed, for such speech conduces to poor writing). Then, with the delivery of a Joan Crawford or a Bette Davis, "And I'd do it again!" Note the exclamation point, so embarrassing but so necessary to convey the scene. Not long afterwards she began releasing her story into the atmosphere to turn friends or acquaintances against me— mutual friends at least.

I sat down with myself in an attempt to see how deeply my hollowness ran. Without being surprised I was nonetheless stunned by the painful slow-motion certainty of a marriage gone down the drain. So this is where even our decreasing momentum must of course lead: to a full stop. There would be all sorts of social reverberations. Undoubtedly there would be professional ones as well. Already Robert Mulligan, whom I represented at the time, phoned with peremptory delight in his voice to ask if what today's *Frank* said was true, that—and here his tone switched to one of moral damnation—my wife had left me after discovering my illicit affair with the publicity manager of a publisher to which I often sold clients' work.

"That is true except in all the particulars," I said. "It is true in the same sense that Gertrude Stein and Alice were transvestites, in the sense that UBC is an internationally important seat of learning, in the sense that Canadians are courteous and Americans peace-loving...."

He interrupted me with the announcement that he had to go. He loves irony, but not in others.

I was trembling a bit as I turned off the phone, closed its little plastic coffin lid and placed it on the desk. Later that same day, Shrink A explained the complex interrelationship between depression and anger. He then went on to say how once one became depressed, there was no telling whether, when or in what form the anger might assert itself. Rage is not unknown, he said. As he jabbered on, I looked beyond his shoulder to the bookshelf containing box after box of old tapes of himself discoursing on the CBC about diseases of the creative personality, a subject on which I am more expert than he, juggling forty clients. That is about the maximum an agent can handle as well as the number below which he cannot get by, and at any one time perhaps fifteen or sixteen of them show signs of serious disorders and disturbances. Yet I am not the one who is tapped to perform analysis, to explain, to interpret on phone-ins, panel discussions or interviews.

My mind was wandering as he spoke. It was out taking a walk in the direction of distemper, and this frightened me more than I would have imagined because it raised the possibility, not to say the likelihood, that my shrink was right and also, coincidentally, that I might be about to come apart from the pain, rejection and stress. I began phoning Cynthia as soon as I got back to my home-office. I mean, I had to warn her about the *Frank* item, even though she wasn't actually identified and if she had been they would have garbled her name and identity so badly as to make her unrecognizable. I had never before phoned her at work. She seemed a bit shocked at first, but then calmed down and listened—listened intently, it seemed to me—as I recounted all the recent events and developments. When I finished, however, she used an angry tone. "If you think I'm going to drop everything to hold your hand while you go through a divorce, you couldn't be more wrong." She actually sounded offended that I had called. I kept talking, hoping to find a smooth way to get off the wire, the way a driver going the wrong way on the motorway pushes on determinedly while desperately seeking some place to cross over to the other side of the divider. By the time I was getting low on fuel, she had moderated her tone. She promised to ring me in a couple of days to see how I was getting along.

How *was* I getting along? As I remember it, I did reasonably well in the daylight hours but then this was during the Toronto winter. At the very least I went through the motions of keeping the agency afloat. There was helping authors shape their proposals. (If they couldn't produce decent book proposals on their own, how could I expect them to turn out manuscripts that wouldn't embarrass everyone into rejection?) That accounted for just some of the meetings with writers who no matter how professional always cling to some of the attitudes associated with the hobbyists who make everyone's life miserable. For years I had accepted invitations to talk at the type of writers' conferences held by community colleges or university continuing studies programmes. Three things could always be depended on to happen. First someone would ask if, in my opinion, creative writing can be taught. I would always reply: Yes, but unfortunately it cannot be learned. My host, the proprietor of some local creative-writing franchise, could be seen wincing in the wings. Then someone would announce with a voice projecting triumph and expecting congratulations in return that he or she was writing a detective story and, get this, the detective was *Canadian*. Then, finally, all the others would speak up and sort of indicate collectively, consensually, unmistakably, but always by the steady revelation of certain silly assumptions and their proofs of ignorance, that they had no intention whatever of writing or learning to write or learning to write better, or even improving their reading, but wanted only to know the alchemical secret of earning big bucks for what they would write if only they chose—memoirs of lives totally without incident, verses, spiritual jottings, accounts of recent holidays both geographical and astral. Surely the key to the other kingdom, the Jerusalem of retirement living, was to have an agent. He, or actually she, for I was one of only two or three male agents once you excluded those who were principally entertainment lawyers or hucksters of some other sort, would know the answer—would have all the answers in fact. This is what the hobbyists believed. Some of the older ones drew their knowledge of literary agents from Hollywood movies and trashy romances in which a writer of heroic genius goes undiscovered until taken up by an attractive New York agent who also solves all the writer's personal problems, including drug addiction, as part and parcel of falling in love with him or her, madly. The point is that this does not accord with my own experience of the agent-author relationship any more than it does with my experience of falling in love with people of any sort. In an ideal world, the task of the agent is simply to solicit offers and advise the client on which one to accept. The point of falling in love, at least in the view of my parents, is to have and rear children. But then they were practically the only ones in the family to survive the war. Doing so, they procreated tearfully, I am sure, and with special determination, and understandably so. This was the *devoir* of Jews their age, the ones who came out the other side alive. Those of us born in the next decade or so have never needed to be told that we were their reward for survival and one of the ways they got through the communist times. I admit it: I don't always have as much patience as the Toronto native-borns or the others drawn to the place seemingly by the same invisible suction by which a river is drawn to the spot on the coast that drains it. I remember that around this time, the awful period between separation and divorce when you cup your ears waiting to learn what sound a *decree nisi* makes, I was walking along Bloor with Eleanor Sims to discuss her nearly finished project and her hopes for it and what she wished to do next.

We passed Spadina walking in the direction of the Colonnade, a favoured spot among the generation before mine, who found it unspeakably sophisticated, no one knows why. On our right was a large outdoor sculpture, a nude female figure with her head buried in her knees, hands grasping her ankles in a position that be could be called seated foetal and seemed to suggest despair. Eleanor nodded at the unremarkable building behind it. "Remember when that was Rochdale?"

"Only vaguely. I've certainly read about it."

"Everybody was always reading about it. It was hard not to read about it. Lurid stories about kids dropping acid and committing suicide from the top because they thought they could fly."

"If they thought they could fly, was it really suicide?"

"It had the same effect in any case." I liked Eleanor's wry little self-confident laugh.

She's a brisk walker too. I remember huffing and wheezing to keep up. I thought for a minute. "Same effect perhaps but a completely different situation."

The next building was the Bata Shoe Museum.

"Toronto will never be the city it thinks it already is until it has a world-class necktie and cravat museum."

Eleanor, God bless her, laughed. I have always used bad comedy to try to lighten the tragedy in my heart. This is my weakness. If I were the protagonist in a novel, the flap copy would describe me as sardonic.

We sat in a pretentious little restaurant in Yorkville. I would never have taken anyone else there, but I knew it was one she liked. She had on an apricot sweater, vastly more attractive than that makes it sound, with a black linen jacket and black wool trousers and black boots. She wore just a splash of jewellery on one wrist.

I pretended to bury my nose in the menu. "I'm having the julienne of kiwi reclining seductively on a futon of rice."

She was always a good audience, or so I thought until that day.

"So how are you bearing up with the Faye business?"

I must have looked startled.

"I've heard about it," she said—sympathetically, I thought.

"Read about it too, I suppose."

"Oh you can't take that stuff seriously. Remember, they said you got me 'a sum not unadjacent to $80,000' for *The Herkimer Delusion*. You and I are the only two people who can prove that's not true."

"The two of us and the folks at McClelland and Stewart."

We had managed to get our drinks order taken but then the waiter disappeared, vanished as in some occult mystery, before we could order food, and this was to have certain consequences.

"She's been on a slightly more even keel the past while, I think. The two lawyers are negotiating back and forth."

"Make sure you've got one who's a good negotiator. All of them aren't, you know." Eleanor, who used to be married to a lawyer, sipped at her Merlot like a bird.

"I feel like now I'm the author and the lawyer's the agent."

I never knew what Eleanor really thought about Faye—they seemed to talk at parties—so I switched the conversation to her project. It was in my interest to be interested, to be intensively involved even while I was zoning out. My eye contact was perfect, I feel, but I was thinking to myself that maybe only patience and perhaps inertia had been holding the marriage together in the face of Faye's Caledonian inability to show affection even in the form of serious conversation.

Aside from constitutional hypochondria, this is Canada's national disease, I believe, despite Atwood's long-ago remark about schizophrenia. For Faye, the turning point was probably the appearance of Gunnar at the right time, just as she gave up hope on me. For me, it was when we stopped trying to conceive. I still think we could have but she just gave up and then the next New Year's Eve told me she really didn't like children. I said nothing, and that was the problem. Being around her, I was losing my own ability to communicate about things that were important. She was turning me into a WASP or a Celt or a goy or whatever term you want to use.

Eleanor and I were quite far into our annual agent/author lunch, but she had finished a second Merlot and I still didn't have any food on my stomach other than a bagel. Ostensibly I was listening to her plans. Inwardly I was ricocheting wildly from anger to grief to relief and felt disengaged from the world that was nonetheless pressing on me hard. She was talking, I remember, and I was being attentive while also lying to myself, trying to raise myself up and bolster myself by lying silently that I am the sort of person who's best in a siege, that I have always been a defender rather than an attacker. The food continued to seem imminent but never arrived, like one of those characters in Chekhov who's forever en route to Moscow.

"It would be reckless hyperbole to say that the service here is manic," I said. My voice sounded odd. We were keeping ourselves alive on a subsistence diet of garlic bread, and the glasses of wine escalated to a litre. Maybe Eleanor was drinking on an empty stomach too; I owe her the benefit of that presumption. The subject got round to the doings of other writers who were common acquaintances, and I began to talk about Blair Estep. I thought they were friendly. Blair was a pretty friendly fellow and was generous to her when she was a guest on his show, I remember. She does well on television. She is one of those people for whom the camera gets a serious hard-on, so it was one of the most mutually successful encounters of the type I had seen.

"Most writers have trouble with the second book," I said. "That's always been the widow. With him it's the third. Maybe now that the show has been cancelled, he'll throw himself back into it and get it done this time, get it right. I know he has been taking it hard. Worried about being out of work all of a sudden. But this could be good for him."

She looked me straight in the eye and said over the top of her oversized wine glass: "He's an even bigger asshole than you are."

I'm not sure how shocked I looked. Our food finally arrived. We ate—without too much haste, I hope. We got up to go. I remember she excused herself to go to the ladies'. Her trousers were perfectly cut with the interesting addition of an extra snugness in the seat to accentuate her bottom nicely. I remember how she looked going across the floor of the restaurant in her expensive boots that gave her a different walk indoors than out. I debated whether to wait and walk with her for a block or so, out of courtesy and a desire for the appearance of normalcy. Acting as though nothing had happened. Was that the proper thing to do at this point? At what stage did politeness turn into a WASP communication failure—repression and sublimation at all costs lest somebody give expression to something more important than weather or gossip? Blair Estep was a friend. Faye liked him as part and parcel of liking Deirdre, his wife. Yet I could hardly stay. Tears were running down my face as though from punctures. I actually felt I might sob, choking, the way I remember doing as a kid when childhood emotions I did not understand and could not even name became inflamed inside me somewhere. So I got my coat and threw my red muffler round my neck and sat down on the chair by the door, not knowing whether to be there or be gone when Eleanor returned from peeing. Which would be less rude, less terrible? I looked out the window. The day was colder now, and it was actually raining slush. Despite several later opportunities, Eleanor never apologised and I suppose I felt I had no way to forgive her. I've once or twice thought that her advice would have been that I go sit in some Anglican church, but of course that wasn't something she could say to someone like me. I was not one of her own. I was not anybody's own.

※ ※ ※

Cynthia did phone back, saying she would be there for me, helping me to get through this time of emotional upheaval. I wondered by what route she had come to this new position, but the answer was not really important to me. I said I'd call her the next evening: it would be my turn then. I heard the awkwardness of the words almost before they were out my mouth, but Cynthia received them in the spirit in which they were offered. I phoned the following night after waiting—this was difficult—until it was late enough on the West Coast for her to have come home from work, rested and had some dinner. This was how I imagined her domestic routine when she was all alone, but I had no way of knowing for sure. So I asked her when I phoned, and we fell into talking easily. She told me how much she loved her "basement suite in Kits", the phrase that still sounded so odd to me. Later, of course, when I started to spend time out there as a regular visitor—rather than as a summer lecturer staying in a hotel for a few days—I realised that in Vancouver all apartments (a word not used on the Coast) are suites, even if they have only one room ("a studio suite"), which to me was like referring to a streetcar as a train. Cynthia asked why we had exchanged so many letters already— didn't I have email? Only for quick replies to business matters, I said; I disliked the medium, though Pam in the office was a computer adept and even supplemented her income by "building" websites for people. Cynthia then began telling me about all the wonderful ways she used electronics. This led somehow to the subject of porn on the web. "Have you ever searched Google groups?" She had a little mischievous giggle as she told me how you typed in your key sex words and they popped up, highlighted, in the texts of story-and-discussion groups, fantasies mostly, literally thousands of them, the Alexandrian library of dirty talk. "Look at the fetishes," she said. "There's a fetish about everything. And everybody. Tonya Harding?" Yes, I knew the name of course: the ice skater involved in that scandal. "There are fetish sites about her. I don't mean porn sites, though there are places where you can watch the sex tape of her honeymoon for free. I mean fantasy stuff." Marsha Clark? She had to remind me who that was: the prosecutor who lost the O.J. Simpson murder trial. "Yup, a fetish object. All these strong women, see." She laughed. She was one of those people whose laugh is far deeper than her speaking voice, making it sound salacious. She said she'd phone me tomorrow night if I was going to be in. "You can depend on it," I said. When we finally got off the phone I was startled to see that we had been yakking again for two and a half hours. I felt happy and alive for the first time in weeks as I lay in bed replaying in my mind the imaginary tape of the conversation. I should have asked her what keywords she liked to search. Breasts? Suck? Anal? I would always wonder. Once we began our nightly phone calls, our relationship was whisked to a higher and much more intimate plateau than before, a loving one in fact. By then I thought I couldn't ask any longer for I was already launched on the process of finding answers to all such questions in the normal course of things, without having to resort to anything so crude as language. Or so I believed. This is how it began: the process by which oral communication slowly came to seem an intrusion on the warm intuitive silence, and in that way started to atrophy.

Even with the psychic lift I got from Cynthia, who after a couple of days made me promise to switch to Sprint as well, I was still severely wounded by what had gone on in Toronto (with worse to come), fearful and wary of what was taking place at that moment and apprehensive about the entire future, the one that would commence in the first second after my realisation of this simple thought. I was thankful Pam was able to take on more of the responsibility without logging any additional hours. The business was slipping through my fingers despite what I believed were my best efforts at trying to concentrate; without her, everything truly would have gone to hell: contracts not returned, letters unanswered, possibly even meetings missed through the simple inability to focus.

There were many highly charged scenes. Faye came by to do her weekly walk with the dog, and I tried to persuade her to take him to live with her in her new home with Gunnar. He was after all her dog, and I was too scattered to care for him as I should, having twice forgotten to let him in after his last run of the night in the tiny fenced-in back garden (once on a very cold night—Pam heard him the next morning and admitted him to the kitchen).

"Don't you think you're just being self-indulgent?"

"You're not the one who's being divorced against, you're the one doing the divorcing."

"You're not going to stand there and tell me this isn't what you wanted all along."

I denied it and resumed talking about the dog.

"Gunnar's allergic to dogs."

Negotiations between the lawyers went slowly over difficult ground. Buy out my half for a reasonable sum, I said; I was happy to take less than the market price divided by two, get out of the Annex and move right downtown, closer to the action, with a set-up where I could live in one room and kitchen attached to a decent-sized office. She had the money to buy me out. A deal like that would take only part of her inheritance. Whereas I pretty much had to liquidate everything else, even RRSPs, to take her half. I understood her desire to start over afresh, but she already had a house she liked, all paid for, renovated to her liking under her direct supervision, and she would be getting a good deal. All right, it was one of the smallest houses in the Annex, if not actually the tiniest, a sort of one-bedroom bungalow set amid the wide-mouthed Victorians, but it was big enough for two as we had shown all these years. As with the dog, I felt the problem was no one's allergic reaction but her own: like the dog, our marital home was covered in my spores, and that made it unbearable, practically unfit for human habitation.

The following week she said she wanted to leave all her furniture and stuff until December at least, a year for God's sake. That night, the phone rang and I was hoping it was Cynthia, but it was Blair Estep. He was full of worthless advice well meant. He said he wanted to remain friends with both of us—the fool. He sounded strange, as though Deirdre were standing behind him, making sure he stuck to the script she had prepared. I started to ask him about his novel but he deflected the question. I was eager to get off the line in case Cynthia was trying to get through. There was nothing smooth about the performance by either member of the cast. I ended up calling Cynthia even though it was really her turn, and we had a wonderfully warm and meaningful talk.

At least that's how it began. Indeed that is how it proceeded for quite a long while until it ended up as phone sex. This was another element of contemporary romance, like Google searches, whose theory I understood but had never actually engaged in before. What a revelation. I got sperm all over the receivables and then she climaxed audibly, her voice going in and out of range and ceasing to be language at all but merely sound. I started coughing. First this was funny, but I got on a real coughing jag and couldn't seem to stop. It happened a second time a couple of days later.

The next time Faye came by to play with the dog, or maybe it was the week after, she refused to speak to me at all, not a word. I assumed she had received through her lawyers the revised offer or perhaps was having difficulties with Gunnar. *Something* was bothering her in addition to the usual Presbyterianism. So I was surprised when the phone rang in the middle of the night—too late for even Cynthia to be calling—and it turned out to be Faye, slightly hysterical, her voice too loud, as though the connection were bad, as on the calls to Europe I suddenly remembered my parents making when I was growing up. She asked if she could come over. When, confused and half-asleep, I said of course, she rang off at once without saying goodbye, as though she at that instant was throwing open her door and flinging herself into the night.

The dog barked in alarm when she rang the bell, then began wagging like a metronome set on maximum once I opened the door. She smelled ever so slightly of liquor, which was definitely never her style, as drinking, if not reined in, could lead to pleasure, and she was a woman to be envied for her self-discipline. There, I'm doing it again. You see how I use humour as a cover, just as the shrink of the first part, a totally humourless man, constantly pointed out to me? In this case I am avoiding another patch of the past that is still raw. Faye said she'd had a call telling her that Blair Estep had killed himself "because his contract was cancelled". She stayed an hour, weeping and smoking, then departed with a silent slam of the door. At that time of night, I was unable to do much except not get back to sleep. Blair—I thought back on all the time we had spent together, both he and I and the two couples. He was the only client who had become a close personal friend as distinct from a business buddy; maybe this was a mistake on my part, but then he was already on his way to becoming a friend when he started publishing and I became an agent. As he was not someone who depended on his writing for food, he didn't produce enough for me to do him much good financially. He was an artist, seeking validation and surcease from pain. Like most writers, however, he never had that one big strike either critically or commercially, but I know he continued to hope, for novelists are the gold prospectors of modern-day Canada, always trying to get together a grubstake, always hoping against hope to discover something fabulously valuable, though Toronto was all staked years ago; claim jumpers were taking over.

Deirdre Estep is a Catholic. I knew that. When they decided to get married, she made Blair convert to Catholicism from whatever variety of Protestant he had been. No doubt he wanted to do so in order to please her. I don't know how he felt about their daughter being brought up a Catholic and going to separate schools. He never betrayed any hint of his feelings about this to me, though I knew his thoughts about most other important developments in his life. Either this was a question so intensely private that he didn't mention it to anyone, perhaps including himself if he could help it, or else it really didn't matter to him one way or another. I have no idea which. We know even our good friends so little. In any case, because of how he died, there was no open coffin for poor Blair at the Catholic "funeral residence", which I'm sure made it more difficult for Deirdre and their daughter and the rest of the family to commune with the spirit or find peace or whatever they are supposed to be doing when they look upon the preserved corpse—maybe it's a type of window-shopping for the Other World. The battered hat he'd taken to wearing the past six or seven years to hide his baldness was lying on top of the coffin, and there was a framed photo of him, smiling and wearing the very hat, on a small highly polished table right next to it. Despite these informal touches, the atmosphere was church-like and I was uncomfortable. Deirdre seemed to be bearing up bravely as far as I could tell, accepting everyone's condolences, including mine, with a clear eye and firm enough handshake, but such things are difficult to gauge; we don't know what's in the bloodstream or how numb the nerve endings are or how unreal—surreal in a way—everything must seem. We cannot know how shocking the shock must really be. I asked if I could call on her later in the week.

A few days later, the cretinous Bob Mulligan came by the office for some reason. Pam was out walking the dog, the part of the office routine she says she enjoys most. Despite the fact that Faye's furniture was still stuffed everywhere, the house had a deserted and unloved feel, which I suppose spilled over into the office portion. This led him to say something about the separation and what he presumed (for he was a presumptuous young man) would be the divorce.

"I always had the feeling about Faye that she was a collector of strays. Maybe you were her biggest catch."

The twit had met her only a few times, surely not enough to theorise about her personality or our relationship to each other. Mulligan not only lacked the sensitivity to be a novelist of any consequence, he also seemed to me, at that moment, to lack enough to be a human. But I let him ramble on until he realised he was not getting a response other than distracted nods and uh-huhs. With equal gracefulness, he moved on to the topic of Blair, who he might have been introduced to once, I don't know, but most likely simply had been reading about in the papers, gloating.

"I bet a lot of people have been killing themselves like that since Mike O. made that bridge famous, right?"

Now I had no doubt whatever that the jerk didn't know Michael Ondaatje either and certainly didn't know him well enough to call him Mike (even I didn't know anyone who knew him that well). I have my doubts that he'd even read *In the Skin of a Lion*. Not his kind of book at all. I responded in my sardonic mode, but hated myself for it afterwards, until I convinced myself that it is sometimes an expression of politeness under pressure, not simply cynicism.

"The reason so many Torontonians commit suicide by jumping off the Bloor Viaduct", I said, "is that they suddenly get depressed after looking at the view."

Mulligan couldn't figure out whether I was joking. His lip uncurled for a moment while he thought about it. Then he concluded that I was. He could not recognize the truth when he heard it.

As for the meeting with Deirdre, it was awkward, as such things are bound to be. She was holding in her grief and humiliation the way a middle-aged man holds in his gut, but with greater conviction. We chatted starkly. She said she wanted to write a Lives Lived about Blair for the *Globe and Mail* but always had found writing anything horribly difficult and this especially so of course. She didn't think she could do it, though it would be nice to have it to send to his family and keep for young Gwen when she was grown up. I thought she was asking me to do it, but I wasn't certain. I muttered something about how Blair had some writer friends but drew widely on people from all walks of life and backgrounds, that's just the sort of person he was: everybody liked him. She resumed the widow's dance, nudging me further towards volunteering, I thought, and so I did. She seemed relieved. I thought I remembered the form of these silly columns, so out of character with the rest of the *Globe* yet the best read feature in the paper, or so one is always told. There is the person's name in bold caps with a head shot of them in their prime. Then, before the few hundred words of text, a few grating lines of italic on the order of this: "Arlene Silverstein, pioneer, mentor, role model, grandmother, great-grandmother and friend, the first woman in Elkhorn, Manitoba, to qualify as a male nurse. Born in Romania, June 1, 1904; died of obsessive-compulsive disorder in Toronto, February 6, 1999, aged 93." The paper insists on including the cause of death. That might prove especially upsetting in this case, though the story of the suicide, and speculation about the reasons for it, already had appeared in the arts section. I asked Deirdre a few biographical questions—parents' names, that sort of thing—scribbling the information on one of the blank pages at the back of my appointment diary.

I saw what she had meant about the difficulty of writing such a thing. Getting it down, getting it right, suggesting the truth accurately while staying within the cornball conventions, and doing all of that in so few words, took far more time and sweat than I had imagined. At one point, in order to concentrate, I had to send Pam out of the office on an errand that was beneath her, especially now that she was taking up so much of the slack around the place, showing so much initiative. Finally I finished it and sent it off. That was a Thursday. I remember because that was the day the psychiatric roof caved in. I sat in that damn little waiting room, waiting of course (how literal—at least *washroom* and the American *restroom* are somewhat metaphorical). Considering the nature of his practice, the doctor could have subscribed to *Descant* or *Brick* or at the very least *Quill & Quire*. Instead I sat there like a person with a toothache, flipping through an out-of-date copy of *Chatelaine* (is there another kind?), past pieces with titles such as "50 Ways to Tell If Your Husband Is Impotent!" and "Sloth: The Silent Killer". When the doctor bade me enter, I thought I detected an ever-so-slight determination on his part to enforce normalcy in a situation that was in no way the norm. I thought I picked up, beneath his distinguished professional demeanour, the slightest trace element of apprehension, so small only a basket case or a dog could detect it. But this may be a trick of retrospect. He told me that he felt he could no longer see me regularly, because he and I had achieved the point (he used the word *apical*) beyond which he could no longer help.

"You're firing me as your patient?"

He replied no, no, that interpretation is incorrect.

I said: "This isn't doing wonders for my self-esteem problem."

He said that he would be pleased to provide the names of several colleagues if I felt I could still benefit from therapy. From that point, the conversation had only a short time to live, particularly after I demanded an explanation. Speaking of colleagues, he went on, he had received a call from my wife's therapist, asking, on behalf of her patient, if he thought I might be given to violent behaviour. That was it. Now it was official. Everyone in town was against me and I must redouble my guard.

Actually there wasn't complete unanimity on this point until the Lives Lived piece came out a few days later (the *Globe* no doubt allowing it to jump the queue because of the news stories about Blair's suicide). I had written that Blair Estep "occupied a place in the honourable middle rank of Canadian writing," neither a literary star or even a major player but rather someone with a strong sense of craft integrity and community. Deirdre phoned me in an absolute rage at what she called my backstabbing, treachery and double-cross. She said she was writing a stiff letter to the paper (I imagined it arriving there on something like the thickness of the cardboard sheets the laundry puts in shirts when it folds them). The following day she called again to discharge the insults that had accumulated overnight. I kept track of the time elapsed: twenty-five minutes to call me an incompetent money-grubbing bloodsucker. I forget the precise adjectives except to say that they were ones in which Father would find anti-Semitic overtones. She said that Blair was always a better friend to me than I was to him, that I betrayed his memory and so on. Very upset indeed. She was naturally enough angry as hell that her husband was dead—and without consulting her presumably. As a result, she was full of wild accusations she needed to release. I have learned that a thick skin is the first requirement of a Good Samaritan. Astoundingly, she called a third time the next day, suggesting that I donate "your fat fee" (it turned out to be $300) to Toronto Catholic Charities. We compromised on a donation to Mount Sinai in his name (she could hardly object). This was not only a way to shut her up, I hoped, but also a sound idea in itself. So with both facts in mind, I volunteered to donate double no triple the fee, which I promptly did. Later in the day, Mulligan phoned to say how much he admired the piece.

The case of the aggrieved widow, however regrettable, should not have been so upsetting a matter, but it was. When I was on top of my game, I was quite inured to many if not most of the insults and abuse on which the cultural life of Toronto is built and based. At least I fancied that I was. Maybe this was an illusion caused by seeing the great toll the world took on clients disgraced by not winning the fashionable awards or any at all, embarrassed by relative penury, ashamed of how they are treated generally. No wonder I was beginning to feel my health wind down. I was cold all the time, couldn't sleep, seemed to have some bad lung infection of the sort I have always been prone to and my collarbone was sore on the left-hand side at the back. My body was rising up against the stress and tension. Cynthia was my only pleasure in life, my only source of hope not to mention simple comfort. I thought about this Blair business a great deal and tried to imagine him entertaining the idea of beginning to contemplate what he eventually would do.

One night I actually thought of not calling Cynthia or pretending not to be home when she called because I was not at all sure I could get it up for phone sex in my condition and was certain she could tell if I tried to fake it. In the event, everything went smoothly in that area, but I was aware I would have to lay off for a few days because, wonderful news, she was coming to visit and I needed all my strength for the real thing.

Faye came by the morning of the day that Cynthia was due to arrive at Pearson and took away two shopping bags of her stuff. Again, she resisted my urgings that we divide the contents now instead of waiting for the divorce to come through, so that she could move out her half of everything all at once. Again, she said that Gunnar had no space. She glowered. In truth, she was using me for free storage. Why should she pay for someplace else? I didn't want to provoke a protracted argument, because I had to go meet Cynthia. I had offered to go to the airport but she insisted on having me pick her up at the end of the subway line instead, because, I assumed, she wished to save me steps or needed a bit of free time to herself, without conversation, to decompress after the flight (I'm that way myself). When I saw her come into the semi-circular waiting area at Yorkdale, I waited for her eyes to catch sight of mine. Her face dissolved into a grin. She was wearing a long tweed coat with a little cape attached, like something Sherlock Holmes might be described wearing, and carrying only one bag and not a heavy one at that. I said to myself: I like this woman. I complimented her on the inverness.

"Second hand. A kind of upscale yard sale. I was lucky. I got there before somebody who would have sold it to a shop as vintage."

"I like your style."

"Hard to think how something like this ended up in Vancouver in the first place. Not exactly a Vancouver coat."

She did a little twirl, Trudeau-like, so that the attached half-length cape billowed up for a second. She wouldn't let me take her bag. "It's not heavy. I figure I won't be needing much." She didn't. We had a lovely time with loving both tender and wild. It was also a weekend full of movie-watching and talk. I remember how small her feet seemed. And how small her voice sounded in the dark when she said, "I've been blessed with a responsive body." The statement was matter-of-fact as well as erotic, though it's one of those sentences that can only sound gauche or ridiculous when set down in unforgiving print. My anxiety about not being up to what she offered proved unnecessary in this case, and I don't know which made me happier, having her there with me or my not humiliating myself with such a woman. We parted full of promises when the weekend was over. She would not let me drop her off at the airport either but called me from there and we talked until she ran out of change for the pay-phone. It was time for her to board anyway. As it was, she was taking the last possible flight that would, if everything went according to schedule, allow her to get to the office without even dropping off her bag at home. Clearly we needed more time, we agreed on that. Until the next occasion, when I'd visit her, we would have our daily phone calls. In fact, two of them most days, one of which always turned into phone sex (I was exhausted). "This is one of the joys of an LDR," she said. I presumed she had had more than one.

What it was that was going on inside my chest only got worse, and drove me to the doctor's. I share my parents' aversion to the medical profession. Actually it's more of a phobia with them, especially with my father, who suffers from a sort of anti-hypochondria, denying the existence of toothache and fractured limbs lest evil doctors use him in their experiments. My fears in this line, though real enough to me and absurd-sounding to others, are less extreme than his and relate mostly to tests rather than treatment. The doctor sent me to the lab for blood work—all standard, he said—and gave me an appointment for the following week. The fact that he didn't phone in the interim suggested an absence of news of the sort that is outright bad. When I returned, though, he told me solemnly that my platelet count was low. He would test again, he said, but then would send me for an HIV test and a marrow test. I was panicky after being slapped by the prospect of mortality this way. I screwed up two big pieces of business, not deliberately but uncaringly, or at least indifferently, as though to say "I've got more important things to worry about now." Eternity issues. I am about to go on eternity leave. Even as I allowed myself to be routed this way, I was aware of how I was damaging myself and others. Yet a deeper stratum of problems underneath numbed me like novocaine and made me actually seek new messes as though to prove I was still capable of any action at all, still part of the world of the living, however dysfunctional a member of it.

The only person I told about the tests was Cynthia—who else could I tell?—and as I did, I started to crash, and loathed myself instantly for doing so. I felt that I was damaging the relationship, letting her know how weak I was when clearly what she valued in me was that I was loving and funny. Yet when I wanted to go on and talk about this very problem or perception, she pulled away with no hesitation. That was maybe the first time I thought to myself that I was making a mistake, not so much in entering into a new relationship before I'd even begun to get over my marriage but rather in trading one of them—WASP, Presbyterian, blonde, Methodist, native-born English Canadian, whatever—for another. "Maybe you should be seeing a therapist," she said in what I could tell was a tone of authentic concern. Having made the mistake of telling her about my tests, I didn't feel I could tell her the whole shrink story, much less the fact that I was now down to only one. It was just too humiliating, too nebbishy, too long and involved, too likely to slow the growth of the positive momentum we had going, or had had going until then. Mistakes, mistakes, messes and mistakes.

I remember pregnant women telling me—who? I don't remember that part—how their swelling bellies seemed to cut off the air in their lungs, leaving them to huff and puff through perfectly normal activities: climbing stairs, for example. I was beginning to feel this way too. I wasn't in pain but my breath was depleted, especially when I thought about it. Was it possible this was all psychosomatic or, more probably, partly psychosomatic? When the weather turned a bit warmer in February I had only very mild distress and *only whenever I remembered to be distressed*, not when respiration problems interrupted my wireless transmissions to myself, so to speak. Surely this was a good sign. Then suddenly I would be overwhelmed by the reality of the situation. Mind over matter, matter over mind, it seemed to alternate.

I was determined I was going to feel better in Vancouver, and I did. Cynthia met the red-eye (this was in the days of Canadian Airlines International, when travel was friendly, convenient and comfortable, even polite sometimes) and I finally got to see more of Kits, as I now knew to call it. Everything was green and mossy outside. Flowers were blooming or just about to. There was an enormous holly tree (she identified the species for me) outside her suite, seen through the glass of the partially below-ground door, which admitted more light than you might imagine. A sliding door in the living room gave onto a series of three steps made with cedar logs (cedar was a species I knew, thank you). You went up these steps and you were in the middle of foliage at street level. I remember, the first time I visited, how surprised I was to see she had a cat, one that was morose as well as especially aloof. "Getting a cat was a major commitment," she said laughingly. At the time I didn't realise what an important piece of self-revelation this was, but perhaps I sensed it. Over breakfast in the morning, we talked about the great loves of our pasts. In her case, her first seemed to have been surprisingly recent. I'm not sure I bought it. Nothing in the story about an LDR. In my case, Faye of course, though I went easy on that because I didn't want to overburden her—part of my fear of losing her by moving too quickly, as her signals (the cat remark, the radio silence about LDRs) were warning me not to do. Also, I wasn't sure I could explain, or even suggest, not without talking far too much, how something that started out with such hope and affection could end in duelling lawyers arguing about the furniture. I wanted to avoid easy parallels with the present.

Cynthia had been hoping for a three-day weekend but found she could not take Friday off after all. I said I'd be fine, I would begin learning about Vancouver not as a rank visitor but as someone who now had an important reason for returning as often as possible: a stakeholder. She went off to catch her bus, the last half-piece of toast still in one hand, soft briefcase in the other.

I spoke to the cat but it spat at me. I looked in the kitchen cabinets. There were those neatly stacked tins of cat food, lots of them, and only a few cans of stuff for humans. The fridge was spotless and sparsely furnished. A carton of skim milk, a carton of juice *beaucoup de pulpe*, two bottles of mineral water, no solid food except low-fat cottage cheese. The bathroom was even neater, as though it had never been used, as though the maids had left only moments earlier or no one really lived in the suite at all. There were lots of hair things but none for the skin (it didn't need any help). The only cosmetic item I found was the plastic bottle of vanilla extract I've already mentioned. The living room I knew. The sort of books she got for free at work, plus a few obviously left over from her university days. I'd seen her bedroom closet once again only minutes earlier when she'd flung it open looking for something to wear. Just as I remembered. No spartan discipline there. Interesting.

I walked down Fourth and figured out how to get onto the Burrard Bridge, remembering Al Purdy's poem about doing night-time sentry duty there during the Second World War, guarding—

successfully, as he always bragged—against invasion by the Japanese. Then I found my way down the other side towards the entrance to Stanley Park. This is the Vancouver everybody thinks they know. Would I come to learn more than the postcards tell? When I thought of my chest I realised I was getting a great deal of exercise with no adverse effects whatever. Was it the temperature that made the difference? Or the fact that I was hopeful and satisfied and certainly more relaxed? Or simply that I wasn't walking uphill or above sea level? Each possibility seemed to me to point to a different diagnosis. Then I thought: Could it be possible that all of this has something to do with being loved, or not being loved, or both simultaneously, in different cities? And though this question was not a question at all but a premonition, Cynthia told me that night that she thought she loved me. I wanted for her to fudge more but she did not. She didn't elaborate, but neither did she fudge.

***

It was March now, the end of March. The lawyers had reached a deal on the settlement. It was basically that I should pay half the market value of the house to Faye, which would wipe me out, and then the lawyers would proceed to the divorce itself. After considerable prodding I got Faye to come over to begin packing some of the medium-sized stuff, too big for shopping bags but still small enough to be carried or at least taken away by car. She was still reluctant, however, to set a date for moving the bigger items with a van. I felt I had to watch her every minute she was there, while she for her part obviously felt I was looking over her shoulder and she just as obviously resented it. She packed the kitchen goods in cartons and then simply transferred them to the cellar. I had to leave for a three-thirty appointment with a publisher downtown. On the way there I saw the new issue of *Frank* with the story of the most recent developments in our impending divorce told from Faye's point of view, quoting exactly her words to me over the phone the night I returned from England. So I telephoned her at home, pretending that the article would be a surprise to her, then asking her to get all her possessions out and thereafter leave me alone. She said she would finish packing tomorrow and would have a van the following Sunday. All the while she kept trying to get even more money—"Do you want this piece for $25?"—even though she had my fresh cheque for all the cash I had in the world. Later (my antidote) I called Cynthia and her voice soothed me as I knew it would do.

Sunday came and Faye and Gunnar turned up in a hired truck. Gunnar, who seemed to be slightly drunk, carelessly piled furniture into the cube, breaking one chair leg. Faye screamed "Oh my God!" and threw her hands up over her face the way melodramatic heroines in the silent movies did. I thought: This is more passion than you've exhibited in years. She was still in tears as the two of them finally pulled away and I was left in merciful but sparsely furnished peace. I would wait, living with an echo, for her to collect herself— I hoped—and in a couple of days phone her at work. She did seem rested and quite a bit calmer. I asked if she might wish to hear some news I had.

"Good news?"

"Well, good news for me certainly—which doesn't automatically make it bad news for you in the least."

She told me to go ahead, so I told her that I was happily involved in a relationship. She naturally asked with whom. When I told her, though, she didn't recognise the name, or pretended she didn't. This suggested to me that she didn't know the identity of the person referred to in the original gossip item months earlier. Then she reverted to habit when facing a situation calling for some exercise of her emotions and merely mimicked an old pop kultch cliché. "Well," she said, "I wish I could say I'm happy for you and wish you both good luck, but I can't and I won't."

I had to explain my reasoning: I wasn't trying to make her feel bad, I only wanted her to hear the news from me first, before it became distorted passing from mouth to mouth like a folk story. She slammed the phone down in my ear. Two hours later she sent me a fax (36-point type) calling me a jerk.

※ ※ ※

Good news, bad news.

Faye had to make one of those necessary phone calls about paper-work, and while she was on the line she volunteered that she was "exhilarated" to be separated and almost divorced from me at last. She seemed to take enormous pleasure in confiding this exhilaration. Then she said an even more curious thing. She said that the separation had sent her into a period of mental illness (her phrase, not mine) for which she was grateful, that it might increase her sympathy for those so afflicted. This blurted-out self-justifying confession struck as me proof, unwittingly offered, of the problems faced by the secular WASP of the species. People like her are not Christians in any religious way, and they look down, from the great eminence of their yoga mats, on those who are. But they are descended from Christians on all sides, surrounded by them as though in a kind of spiritual massacre, and will occasionally give voice to some embedded Calvinist imperative without even being aware that they are doing so, like old Marxists who long ago lost their ideology and never stop to consider why they're still wearing denim shirts that reveal their solidarity with workers who no longer exist.

I remember this so vividly because the same afternoon I also took calls from the two people who had now become the most important in my life: Cynthia and the doctor. Cynthia and I fell to discussing how we could be together every day. That is, which one of us would pick up and move? We both knew the answer. There were certainly more publicity manager jobs in Toronto than in Vancouver and what's more they changed regularly through the inexorable process by which the most talented publicists get promoted, often beyond their ability or at least their interest, to marketing manager when the previous occupant moves along to the next publisher. This life-cycle creates openings for another generation of young women for the publishers to exploit, "like a forest fire making way for new growth" in Cynthia's phrase. At the moment she was perhaps stuck as the number two marketing manager in Vancouver publishing with nothing else to aspire to. Number one was not about to leave anytime soon. People twelve or fifteen years younger were scurrying round her ankles like mice paid twenty-four thousand a year to squeal. I could move the agency to Vancouver. The publishing scene was large and lively but with only two or at most three big players, all of them regional, and a couple of local agents serving them already. My impression was that there wasn't any money to be made except by selling West Coast authors to the big Toronto publishers I was dealing with, the ones who were my bread-and-butter. In moving there I would find only writers looking for a Toronto agent, which I would have ceased to be. Of course I could have commuted regularly but that would perpetuate the inconvenience of the LDR, with one or the other of us always flying from YVR to YYZ or the other way round. With this kind of candid pragmatism sprinkled with erotic phrases, Cynthia and I reached the decision: she would move in with me in the former matrimonial home sometime around the end of the summer or the early autumn. My heart was full.

For obvious reasons, she had delayed going into work that morning so she could have this conversation privately. No sooner had I let her go, reluctantly, than the doctor phoned, saying he had been trying to reach me. That's one of those phrases that you really dread encountering, like "Your teeth are fine but we need to talk about your gums" or "Chinese and Canadian Dishes Our Specialty". He told me that the lab had bungled the most recent specimens; we were back to square one and I would need to be retested. I said fine. To myself, however, I resolved to get a second opinion, ideally from someone who inspired a bit more confidence, even before the first opinion was in. Toronto was experiencing an especially balmy early spring. On days when I seemed to have my old lung power back, I attributed the improvement to a change in the weather that was beating up a resilient infection at last; when I had a bad day, I worried but delayed taking action, telling myself repeatedly how suggestible I am (and how repetitious).

I was wrecking my business through neglect both benign and malignant, but I was confident it would right itself once Cynthia and I were living together. In the back of my mind I even held out hope that she would come in with me once she felt more comfortable in the East: in this and in other ways, I thought, we would be a good team. In any case, once she made the decision to move, we grew ever

more passionate. Turning all the pending contracts and correspondence (and the dog) over to Pam, who responded neither one way
or the other, I boarded the red-eye and went west for five days.
Vancouver taxi drivers were staging a job action at the airport so
although it was three in the morning when I arrived I was met by
Cynthia who was wearing the cape-coat—with only an emerald-
coloured satin chemise on underneath, as she showed me with a
flash before we were out of the terminal. We made love in the morning, the real morning I mean, with rain pouring insistently, then lay
there, in the sterile neat room with the nonetheless overstuffed closet,
talking of the future, the timing of the move (probably before Christmas,
she felt now) and her birthday in two days' time. I asked her what
she wanted, reminding myself as I did so how Faye had answered
the same question. "I want you to help me throw a party," Cynthia
said. "Don't worry. Just a small one. No publishing people. No business talk. Old friends only." So we spent the next day walking the
other Seawall, the one on her side of the water, and going to one of
the delicatessens in Granville Island Market. (I remember thinking
back to when shopping together was a romantic activity for Faye
and me as well, though recalling it, only to myself of course, did not
make it easier to believe.)

"When my parents first came to Canada," I told her, "we used to
go down to Kensington Market in Toronto. Do you know what I
mean? Well, the TV show cleaned it up a bit, shall we say. It was this
wonderfully dirty old place, sort of hidden away, that every group
of immigrants had used as a holding area before they were assigned
neighbourhoods of their own, so to speak. Each one left a little
something behind. It's mostly Chinese now, like Spadina, but it
used to be Greek and Portuguese and Italian. Before all that it was

Jewish. My parents felt comfortable there, all the more so because it was also a little like an English market, with splintered wooden crates and rotten fruit, sometimes escaped live chickens being chased up one of the lanes. There was still a synagogue, though it's been a lot of other things since then; I think it's some sort of Korean social service agency now, or was the last time I looked. There are still a lot of old houses where you can see the mezuzah next to the front door under layer after layer of paint." Then to myself: Ah, I see. "It's a Hebrew prayer on a slip of paper that's wadded up inside a little metal thing attached to the front of the house." We went on, talking talking talking.

The miniature birthday party at the basement suite was odd or rather the guests were. They run together in my memory now, thus opening the way for exaggeration, but it seemed to me they were flakes, kooks to use my parents' favourite purely North American word, which they may like because there is supposedly no precise Yiddish equivalent (though I find that hard to accept given *meshugoyim*—my parents, who spoke Hungarian and German in eastern Hungry, also had enough Yiddish to believe, mistakenly, that they could keep me from eavesdropping on sensitive conversation). I remember there was a woman at the party who had lived on a sailboat with her then-husband, sailing round the world, but was now—can I be remembering this correctly?—"a personal shopper for dogs". Evidently she went to the homes of pet-owners with busy careers (this would be on the North Shore, I know now) and interviewed their dogs about their favourite chew toys and personal preferences in organic, low-fat treats and went and shopped on their behalf. Another woman believed strongly that evidence obtained through séances should be admissible in Canadian criminal trials. The men were no saner. Through her acquaintances

I began to see a side of Cynthia I hadn't known existed and was now a little frightened of. I asked her about this later and she said that when she was with me she used the eastern side of her brain but with her local friends, the western. Somehow this didn't reassure me. My chest started to hurt, but that was probably just because of the after-dinner pot smoke, I said to myself. But I had one more small flare-up, nothing to worry about, when I returned to Toronto. This I put down to tension, of which there was indeed so much in my life in those days. Sometimes it quivered in the distance like heat on the desert horizon.

These visits back and forth accomplished quite a lot besides merely satisfying our mutual need to see each other in and out of bed. Each of us was taking a crash course in the other. She spoke of her vexed relations with her parents, who divorced when she was quite young, a few years before her mother's death, I think. She asked me straightforward questions that were difficult to answer in the same spirit but needed to be asked all the same.

"Do you think of yourself as less Jewish than your parents?"

No, I said quickly. Then, speaking very carefully, I tried to explain how although less observant (except I sometimes seem to be very observant in order to please them), I'm as much a Jew as either of them though important generational differences come into play. "For my father especially, being a Jew has always been a full-time job." Going on far too much, I then told her about how he would sometimes get when he wasn't feeling well. "He got a parking ticket in North Toronto and pointed to it on the windscreen and told me that the paper was the same shade of yellow on the yellow star." Then to be absolutely sure of my audience: "…that the Nazis made Jews wear."

"If we had a child, would you want him or her to have a Jewish education? I know she wouldn't be Jewish because I'm not, but wouldn't you feel better knowing she would be able to make decisions about her heritage and what to be proud of?"

I swear I couldn't keep from choking up. Real tears were about to appear. She was becoming emotional too. She told me she was thinking of moving up the time, formerly two years in the future, when she'd want to have a child. We had crossed some invisible line together and in doing so had closed a gap. At that point I hadn't realised how moving dates forward and back was the result of ambivalence, fear and I don't know what else. I began to wonder what she must be like in a work environment, but then neither of us was behaving with good business sense. We couldn't afford the time to go off together somewhere for an extended period and so we were ruining our professional lives and emptying our bank accounts one bit at a time by flying across the country for cramped weekends. I was not sure how long this could go on. So far, she had not even begun moving in the way Faye had moved out: one small object at a time. She never left so much as a toothbrush behind after one of her Toronto visits. I noticed, in fact, that her luggage, never large, got smaller with each trip.

Her turn to visit coincided with some social events at which I thought we should appear together now that Faye was fully cognizant of the relationship. Quite apart from the question of future domestic arrangements, it would be good for us to be seen as a couple. She said she craved Vietnamese food (to me, the only Asian cuisine of no interest whatever, as though cooking had prophesied the American intervention). But the place she chose was better than I had expected. After the meal, we made our way to Robert Mulligan's loft on Adelaide to attend a party he was holding as a fundraiser for PEN. Mulligan obviously was hoping to use his prehensile tail to climb up the organisation, getting into the orderly rotation by which he would eventually serve a term as president. If achieved, this would represent quite a feat of sucking up, for so far as anyone knew he had not gone to private schools or even an elite university but only to some place with a name such as Corner Brook Community College; and PEN, or its Canadian expression at least, was above all a body of upper-middle-class white kids doing good in the world by sipping white wine to end oppression. The fact that as recently as a year earlier Mulligan had been a kind of pro-censorship activist, writing in the *Globe* about his desire to destroy art works that offended him in commercial galleries, would be forgotten.

His loft was dark and cavernous and filled with people standing shoulder to shoulder as in a crowd scene in a movie. One of the first people we ran into was Eleanor Sims, looking stylish and intelligent as usual. She was doing her hair differently. It was just as blonde but shorter and cut on the bias, sweeping down across her forehead from northeast to southwest, like a wedge-shaped field of very expressive wheat. She looked and sounded great. When I made introductions, she was perfect. No polygraph, however sensitive, would have betrayed the slightest reaction or appraisal, but I thought I could hear her thinking "Ah, so you're the one" as she shook Cynthia's hand. What she said aloud, however, was "Have you seen the chandelier?", her eye motioning to the ceiling where there were metal rings, hooks and hoists. "The leader of the Queer Newfie Renaissance", she said sweetly, "is deeply committed to political prisoners." Her eyes twinkled.

I don't think Cynthia liked her. So later I told her the story of how she had called me an asshole to my face and ignored every opportunity to apologise, an incident, I said, that would have been even more hurtful than it was if it hadn't come when the Faye business was at its worst, or what I hoped was its worst. (*Was*, past tense, though significantly, two people at the party cut me dead, one actually turning on his heels when I spoke to him.) Later that night, back at my place—soon to be our place, I thought with a serotonin rush—she let drop that her September move-in was now put back to October. But this turned out to be her attempt to break to me gently the news that in fact it had been extended "six months to a year after that". This announcement toppled me off into a depression that she later said lasted three days (felt like one day to me, one really bleak day of mental and physical immobility). Of course, she was back home by then, so much of her diagnosis was done over the phone. In any case, even by my version of the chronology, it was a black time full of tears and temper. She became moody, demanding and condescending. The visit ended with a drink at Terminal Three the next night before she boarded her flight.

We agreed that I would skip a visit to the Coast. I simply had to catch up on my work: now clients *and* publishers were threatening to wash their grubby hands of me, provoking a mess that I could scarcely blame on the Faye business. Cynthia was still set to return for a longer stay the following month, round the time of the Canadian Booksellers Association convention where she could hunt for a job in Toronto, but by then I knew she would rethink this plan too if we didn't communicate enough, and meaningfully enough, in the interim.

There was a day the following week, I remember, when I had six communiqués from her—letter, voice, email—none of them with the old passion, though she continued to say she loved me. In one of the phone calls, she said she had been suffering from PMS when we argued earlier, but a man never knows when that is being used as an excuse, an apology or just an explanation and really can't enquire any more closely. I tried to work out the calendar time since her previous period, but as the figures were imprecise, the arithmetic was inconclusive. Thinking about the matter, however, I was forced to confront the real subject of my fear, or one of them. That loopy birthday party had been in commemoration of her thirty-seventh. She had never had kids. As far as I knew, in fact, she had never actually lived with a man, ever. She admitted she was experiencing what she called the womb-twitch. I'd never heard the phrase before but was certainly acquainted with the phenomenon. In any case, some credence was lent to the PMS statement by the way her disposition improved over the next few days. I started to feel better too. Hardly a coincidence of course. Then I thought to myself: Maybe she's jollying me along because she feels this is necessary to securing my services as the father. Then I started to slide under the psychological covers once again. While down there, I had an equally disturbing thought, a realisation actually: that to judge by the most recent experience, we were doing much better on the phone than in person. And what did it mean that I was the most aware of my chest whenever matters in the other compartments of my life weren't going well?

CBA, as Book Expo was still being called in those days, always takes place in June. Cynthia came with two bags this time, one medium sized, the other small, in acknowledgement of the longer duration and also the fact that she was to begin job-hunting now. She seemed to set about the task with sincere dedication, and quickly had a couple of nibbles, for most everyone in publishing dreams of leaving the micro-managed rat-pits of Toronto for the leisurely life of the Coast, not the other way round. That week was one of equatorial heat, real sticky-vest weather. So much so that Cynthia suggested we give up on the bedroom and relocate in the almost-finished basement where it was cool. So we ended up in subterranean splendour, surrounded by Canadian Tire panelling, sleeping atop not inside two sleeping bags placed on thick mats. The dog came down as well, seeking company but also the spot near the hot-water tank where the indoor-outdoor carpet had been taken up, I forget why, so he could sleep with his bare belly touching the cool concrete. He didn't have to be asked to go upstairs when we decided to make love, however; he naturally wished to excuse himself, going up the steps with a galloping motion. Cynthia said she was ovulating. Ah yes, the relationship had reached the basal thermometer stage I remembered. I was able to perform satisfactorily, though my fatigue was deep (the heat hadn't helped). As soon as we finished she rolled up her sleeping bag, piled her pillows on top of the roll and lay down on her back with her head flat on the floor and her feet quite elevated. I couldn't keep from asking whether this had any scientific basis as an aid to conception; I found it funny that anyone would believe the spermatozoa would slide to their destination more smoothly aided by mere gravity or that if inverted they would fall out, like coins from a pocket. Cynthia smiled and said she wasn't taking any chances.

"An old wives' tale, perhaps, but those old wives were pretty sharp, you know. That's how they got to be old grandmothers."

The next day the heat let up and we took the dog for a much longer walk than I was usually able to manage, indeed much longer than he got even from Pam. We let him run free in the ravine behind Sir Winston Churchill Park. We walked on the steep grassy hillside on the north side of the park and along the flat trail down below, all the while trying to keep an eye on the dog. When we realised he had disappeared again, we started calling his name as loudly as we could, or as loudly as we dared. Soon there would be a clumsy rustling in the bush before his big face emerged from the saplings, like an actor sticking his head through the opening in the curtain to look at the audience. He'd have one ear up and the other down and his tongue hanging out the side of his muzzle; he looked happy and dishevelled and filthy. I got Cynthia to talk seriously but calmly, never an easy matter, about the way her desire for maternity had returned. Then I teased her about how she chose the prospective father. She said without hesitation, "Whoever steps up to the bar." We were both convulsed with laughter for a moment.

We decided to cook in and get videos for later. The kitchen cupboards were mostly empty now, though Faye had left me the third of every vessel and utensil of which we had had three. Cynthia and I could not help but joke about the strange assortment of stuff: mismatched wooden salad fork and spoon but no salad bowl, no spatula but two whisks, the inside but not the outside of a salad spinner (now renamed the colander).

"This is like being in a rented cabin," she said. "A very empty and poorly furnished rented cabin."

She was wearing a plain white apron that Faye never liked; it made whoever wore it look like an elderly waiter in a German beer garden. She found various kinds of pasta in tall jars, only one of which looked as though it held enough for two, and I went out for veg and bread. I hadn't been eating at home much nor eating much when I was out; I found that eating too much, which I'd do if I wasn't paying attention, sometimes made my chest twinge a bit. We worked together well, moving round the small kitchen in our self-assigned tasks, never bumping into each other but occasionally grabbing at the other person erotically, playfully.

We'd got two movies, and I used my host's prerogative to force mine on her as the first choice, suspecting that I might not be awake for all the second.

"You're sure you've never seen this?"

She said no.

"I can't believe I'm getting to introduce you to *Sunday, Bloody Sunday.*"

"The title's familiar."

"One of the seminal British films of the sixties. In fact, this *is* the British sixties. It's certainly the way London was when I was growing up. No high-rises yet. Watch for the minis. That's what the streets were full of." I elaborated quickly: "The cars."

We ate and watched, sitting on the smaller sofa left behind, the TV and VCR resting on phone books on the floor.

"Can you believe Glenda Jackson? Of course everyone's good-looking in their thirties."

I realized this was perhaps an impolitic thing to have said, but it seemed not to soak in. She was only a child when the film was released. To her, this was archaeological cinema set in a place about which she had no curiosity whatsoever, unlike the native-born Toronto people my age who made pilgrimages there honouring the British Invasion or something. Contrary to the advertising pitched at bringing American dollars to Victoria, British Columbians are the least British people in the Commonwealth, knowing nothing about the UK except that they're supposed to hate it. In my peripheral vision I could see Cynthia honestly trying to figure out what I was making such a fuss about.

"Watch this. This shocked people in those days more than you could possibly imagine."

But she saw nothing in the least remarkable about Peter Finch giving his boyfriend a long lingering kiss on and in the mouth. In Vancouver, everybody one is ever likely to meet is bisexual, gay or lesbian, though there are aggressively straight people in the Interior and other regions, I am told.

There is a point in the film where Glenda Jackson complains that her lover (the one she shares with Finch) must be "bludgeoned into feeling something". I looked over to see if the words made Cynthia as uncomfortable as they did me.

❊ ❊ ❊

In the summer, when it finally stops raining and the sun comes out at last, Vancouverites leave town so as not to be weakened by pleasure or even comfort. So Cynthia was not unusual in the least. She saw nothing odd about this. For as long as she could remember, her family had had a fishing cabin on a lake in the Chilcotin. I once made the error of calling it a cottage, which I have to admit it is not, and locating it "up north" when one would need go quite a bit higher up the map to attain even the bottom reaches of that particular geographic abstraction. She was eager to depart as soon as her holidays began in a few days' time. The most important difference between British Columbia and Ontario is that BC is outdoors. I suppose she wished to see how a Jew, and a potential father, might function in the wild.

The day of departure arrived, and I used Cynthia's computer at home to check in with Pam one last time and then we were away. She was peeved that we were not leaving until eleven in the morning, but it wasn't my fault we were late; she too had many last-minute items to attend to. Once we got out of the city, though, her mood reversed itself, and she seemed to take great delight in explaining things to me, as seemed perfectly natural; she was the host after all. We were on what she called the old route, through Whistler. As co-pilot, I was the keeper of the map, and the farther up on the map we went the more deserted hay barns and old ranches we saw. Immense granite strata by the verge are the other thing I recall. One stretch of the highway, forty or fifty kilometres perhaps, was mere gravel, populated every so often by flag-girls, as they are evidently called. The flag-girls are usually young and flaxen-haired and deeply tanned, wearing steel-toed boots that seem impossibly large for them and have rawhide laces wrapped round the tops several times. Despite this, some of these young women are able to execute a sort of dance step when they move about, no doubt to keep their circulation flowing and the boredom in check. I remember the general store at 100 Mile House as quite the most thoroughly general I had ever seen. The temperature was approaching forty degrees. Cynthia's car had no air conditioning. We had the windows rolled down and were panting audibly like a pair of hounds.

Somewhere before 150 Mile we blew out a tyre. Cynthia handled the situation coolly and efficiently. We waited amid wildflowers—blue, yellow and burnt orange, their names unknown to me—for the BCAA to arrive and change the tyre. Then we went to Williams Lake on the spare, bought a new one, had the wheels realigned, and shopped for supplies. It was nearly seven when we rattled down to the end of a path that was like a minor tributary of a winding unpaved road and saw the cabin perched on the shore of a lake that was itself like a large and sudden clearing in the bristly wilderness. She told me, needlessly of course, that being there made her feel both happy and sad. At the time, I assumed this referred to the family's emotional business; now I'm not so sure. She said she wanted to spend some time alone on the water before the sun began to withdraw. We were both tired and I at least was stiff in my joints.

In the morning, we cleaned the cabin together, knocking down the cobwebs from the corners and sweeping the plywood floor. The little stove was for heating, not cooking, so Cynthia made a fire outside, inside the circle of rocks still intact from long ago, and I made us breakfast. The cabin was one of those places whose smell you can guess accurately from photographs, and it was full of stuff. I sensed the place served the function of an estate, with each member of the family expected to keep it repaired and ready for the next, which in this case, I realised with an exclamation point, might be our daughter or son! We went through the inventory of food and medicine, discarding any items too old to use (food in the car to go to the dump in the next town, medicine down the outhouse). Then we took some of the new food and picnicked on the tiny dock. She said this was the first time she remembered it being hot enough to swim in the lake: "Global warming." So saying, she looked round to where no one could possibly be, took off everything except her knickers and wriggled into the water. She swam with perfect ease and confidence. She was doing the breast stroke and each time she pushed her arms away from her body she created a fan-shaped design on the surface, like the wake of a silent steamship on still water in the moonlight. She swam with a smile on her face.

Over the next couple of days, she taught me new words, pointing to whistle pigs on the ground, cupping her ears to the sound of whisky-jacks in trees. She said that as I did not know the history any more than I knew the flora or fauna, we should go to Barkerville, though it was quite a distance to drive. The province had started restoring its dilapidated false-front buildings and board footpaths not all that long before she was born, and her family had taken her there quite a few times when she was growing up. Each year there were more tourists, she said, but each time a bit more had been reclaimed from oblivion for them to see: such was the cause and effect. A holiday should have enough flex in it to accommodate the occasional whim, she said; this was not some time-share scheme we were locked into; she wanted to show me Barkerville and dammit she would show me Barkerville. The next day we closed the cabin for the summer and packed the car. Of course, she was simply trying to teach me that there was more to BC than Vancouver, a place people elsewhere in the province often view, silently, with a suspicion similar to that with which Vancouverites, audibly, almost piercingly, view Toronto. She was checking in on her own past again, making sure it was all right. A part of nest-building, I thought.

We took about four hours to get there. We threaded our way back to the gravel road and the minor highway, then onto the major one, heading north. The implied history lesson was successful to this extent at least: I couldn't begin to imagine how people got into this country before there were roads. The enormous sky seemed a cruel tease, for the landscape on all sides appeared impenetrable in a way that was almost arrogant, and this was the height of the summer, mind you, and only the pretend North.

"The best part of Barkerville is three or four kilometres before you get there." She went on to explain about Wells, another mining town but of a different era and one that had never quite died, even though the mining had. "When I first went to work at the press, there was a woman who was just leaving. I wasn't replacing her; it was a coincidence. We overlapped for maybe a week. I really liked her. You know how sometimes you meet somebody and know right away you could be friends? She moved up to Wells to write. I've even seen some stories in journals and little mags but I don't think she's published a collection yet. Not as far as I know. We've tried to stay in touch but you know how it is. The last card I had said she'd rented an old church and was living there." I remembered the two lesbian artists in the Robertson Davies novel who lived and worked in an old Toronto church. Like so many of his characters, they were instantly recognisable to Ontario people of a certain age. Eleanor Sims' mother, for example, had been acquainted with them.

Wells was like a little spot left high and dry when a mighty river was diverted from its original course and the water rushed off in a new direction. In this case, the riverbed was the highway that carries the tourist coaches to Barkerville and back. The principal street, the only street with commerce on it, was circular, hugging the edge of a large tumulus of what I suppose was waste matter from the mine or mines. Numerous holes in the town plan, like spaces on a broken comb, indicated where additional buildings had stood. On the basis of the ones that remained, imagining what they looked like was easy enough. There was a tiny box-like general store with a false front. Directly opposite, dwarfing the other enterprises in town, was an old hotel that had obviously had a lot of money pumped into renovations. Next to that, however, clinging precariously to the outside of the circle as though thrown there from the centre by centrifugal force, was an abandoned shop in a state of such unpainted abandonment that it listed dangerously and was reached at all only by a bare weathered catwalk over a deep ditch and the catwalk too looked unsafe, as though a foot placed on it however delicately would crash through the rotted planks.

There was a steeple showing round the curve of the roundabout. On closer inspection it turned out to be an art gallery. A woman my age or older, dressed like a Ukrainian peasant of the Stalinist era, complete down to the head scarf and shapeless cotton skirt, appeared and introduced herself in a friendly fashion. I took her for another refugee from the metropolis, though perhaps not so comparatively recent a one as the missing acquaintance, whom Cynthia named and described.

"And she writes stories for children?" the woman said.

"No, not for children, not as far as I know."

"I think she used to work at that one." And she pointed unequivocally to another church. "Wells used to have three churches," she said with pride. "Now all of them are studio-galleries." Her pride increased. Evidently Wells was once a thoroughly Christian community, I said but only to myself, though now looks elsewhere for its spirituality and also profit perhaps. This surely was a step forward. How would I feel if the churches were three former synagogues like the one in Kensington Market? Differently no doubt.

The missing person, we learned, had been connected to the last of the three, where she made and sold silkscreen tee shirts.

"In a place like this, everyone has more than one job," the owner explained, but obviously more for my benefit than for Cynthia's. (Did I really look so different from her, age aside? Not in how I was dressed surely.) "In the summer, most people work in Barkerville, not as guides necessarily but just walking around in Victorian drag. Sometimes there's work at the hotel, working for the Germans."

It seemed that German immigrants owned that particular place and some others as well.

Our mission was a failure. As we'd been driving so long and dining opportunities in Barkerville were limited, I was told, we decided to have lunch at the hotel, where we were served by a thin aesthetic-looking individual for whom a career in the hospitality sector was clearly not a long-term goal. And there in that dining room something started to take place that I have been trying to properly analyse ever since, always as part of a large life-mess, though an important part, I believe, and usually in those hours before falling asleep or just after waking that are the dusk and dawn of consciousness.

Cynthia said how she would have liked to have met up with her glancing acquaintance again and hoped she had not given up writing. This led to further reminiscences of her own early days at the press. Which led to an argument about the purpose and value of small literary publishers—as they insist on calling themselves when in fact most are as commercially minded as the big international publishers but with no clout and almost no resources.

The discussion went something like this. I said that the small press and the private press (a term you don't hear much except in the circles of book collectors and craft-printers) were Victorian in origin and served legitimate functions in that society but that the functions had been eroded, not to say corrupted. I could sense her starting to bristle at that—misunderstanding me, I thought—so I was careful to explain what I meant. This was evidently an error.

"In Europe and England, America too, there was suddenly a great new reading public—mass literacy—and new technology to supply the demand. The Industrial Revolution's effect on culture. Are you with me?"

Those were my words. Looking back, of course, I suppose she considered them condescending. Certainly they sounded a bit like lecturing. But I was only trying to figure out what, in broad terms, she knew already, so I wouldn't give offence by belabouring the obvious. Looking back some more, I realize that one of our problems was an age difference just big enough so that we were not sure how much cultural luggage we had in common. Not just pop culture, which changes so quickly, but the general ideas we are injected with in classrooms. She looked at me with such scepticism that I had to continue with the thought simply to put it on the agenda, so to speak.

"Suddenly—it must have seemed sudden—the working classes in England, let's say, could read (and vote). To those in power, it was important that they not be exposed to ideas that would encourage any further change. The system was very paternalistic. The established order had its own self-interest in mind, of course, but it also thought it necessary to protect the less fortunate, the less sophisticated."

She was trying to be patient, I could see that, but I was in fact coming to the point.

"Here's the point," I said. "Erotic books, for example, were only for the wealthy and educated who wouldn't be perverted by them. I know, but that was the thinking at the time. So you had publishers like Leonard Smithers. His name always comes up in books about Oscar Wilde or Sir Richard Burton. He published both of them. Because his books were privately published—not for sale in shops, and not through the post (an important point)—he could get away with stuff. People like that encouraged the illusion that their books were available only by subscription. To gentlemen."

"So some old pornographer invented the literary press scene? Is that the kind of thing you're telling me?"

"Of course not. Let me finish, okay? The avant-garde—early modernism—was the same situation." I had the feeling I should have skipped Smithers and gone straight to the moderns. "The educated who were sophisticated—middle-class now, not aristos—had to protect the educated who *weren't* sophisticated from what they didn't understand while getting it out to people like themselves, spreading the word, gaining acceptance. Young aesthetes whose money came from fathers who had made it in Sheffield steel and wouldn't understand all this damn nonsense, you see? Again, limited editions, small presses, private presses: the same conceits but a different purpose. Mostly different anyway. Sometimes there was still the legal problem to take into account. *Lady Chatterley's Lover, Ulysses* and all that."

"I know all that. I went to university. In this country."

Damn, I knew I'd made a hash of everything. What made me not change the subject? I felt as though I was stepping off the kerb into the path of a speeding omnibus with no one to grab me and pull me back at the last second. Maybe I was also afraid of silence. A terrible thing, silence. Fear of it is what permits old phoneys like the literary shrink to clog up the airwaves with his fluent opinions on an endless roll, to be pulled out like loo paper. You might suppose in this case that I would have been associating dead air with anger. In this case, that would have been the easier interpretation, but I mean the type of anger people seem to be born with, the kind I associate with rigid Protestantism. Instead, I blundered on, but I did so in a spirit of calm, in a friendly tone, I believe. Faye used to call this my negotiating voice.

"There was still a logic to this in the sixties and seventies. Presses like Coach House and House of Anansi were trying to create an audience for writers the big publishers wouldn't touch because they didn't have track records. When they got track records, then they were lured away and got decent money sometimes. Thanks in part, I might say, to people like me. We also did most of the work getting publishers outside Canada for the lucky ones."

She hit the roof. She really lost it. Her voice stretched out like a thin wire.

"Finding the new writers is what we're supposed to do. When we've given them confidence and the kind of attention they couldn't get from anyone else, then they move on, most of them. There's always a new generation right behind them, though. Geez, can't you see that? It's always been this way."

I started to agree with her but she cut me off.

"A lot of excellent writers are published by presses like ours their whole careers, as you very well know. They can't get the same quality of publishing anywhere else. Then there are the ones who become important international writers—I'm thinking of Atwood, Ondaatje—but always still support the independents any way they can. They're loyal to their roots. What about them?"

Now a note of real defiance had insinuated itself into her voice.

"I agree that's admirable," I said. "The entire book trade knows how important the real literary presses are. No one disputes that." Here I began to sound a bit defensive, I suppose. As I reconstruct the events now, this is when I let my negotiating voice return to its hiding place. "All I'm trying to say—the point I'm coming to—is that most of these little companies [that was a phrase I could see didn't go down well—was it *little* or *companies*?] haven't been literary presses for years. They still publish poetry and fiction but it's mostly by people the Randoms and the HarperCollinses won't touch and never will."

If I could have seen her from the rear, I'm sure the hair on the back of her neck would have been erect. She'd made eye contact and was refusing to let go; was locked on her target.

"No, really, I mean it. Let's be realistic. Small publishers, and I'm *not* talking about your group or anyone in particular really, are scrambling to find specialties they can exploit. Rock music books, books about New Age medicine or the occult—or local history about their region. There's usually one owner, a small-time entrepreneur…"

She interrupted to say *co-operative, collective* and *not for profit* but couldn't offer many examples.

"…who has a small base income from grants."

She was furious.

"His salary is in the application as 'administration'. It's not much maybe, but he can depend on it. Grants also pay the printers for the most part. If he sells any poetry or fiction, it's a bonus. But it doesn't matter. And most of his time goes into struggling to sell the same kind of trashy non-fiction a lot of the big foreign publishers do much better. The difference is he can't afford to pay for it and hasn't got the marketing clout to blanket the trade with it. In the meantime, he's used up a great deal of energy he should have been putting into Canadian writing—developing Canadian writers, I think we both agree."

Here I thought I was back-pedalling attractively, but Cynthia said: "Don't tell me what you think I'm thinking!"

Our voices had obviously escalated more than I'd noticed. There were one or two stares. I got the bill and paid it, and we walked back to the car. Only to continue the argument as she sped round the town circle to the highway and raced off in the direction of Barkerville once more. There's always a worse feeling to leaving an argument unfinished than to letting it play itself out. Forensically but emotionally as well. We were still so polite, though, that each of us waited for the other to resume. Finally, as I uttered the first syllables of what would have become a sentence, she beat me to it. We were like a pair of people trying to pass each other in a narrow corridor, Person A stepping to the left at the same instant Person B steps to the right, and so on, several times in succession.

"You're talking like an agent."

"That's what I am. Working to do the best I can for my clients."

"You get some charge out of making deals and having lunches. It's some kind of a big-dick thing." I almost laughed. "If you had your way, there would only be the ten biggest companies publishing the same twenty-four writers over and over."

"That's ridiculous."

"You won't work with the independents."

"They won't spend money to get the books that sell. But then why should they? It doesn't matter to them what sells so they publish what doesn't and needn't do, and they're subsidised anyway. Also, they get it for free. It's rather a sweet deal actually. Of course to be fair they do not, as a result, *have* any money to spend for anything different." I said the independents felt the fact that a book was free, aside from the expense of a little flattery for the poor benighted author, was a big mark in its favour and that their values had therefore become distorted. And when a book did sell well through no effort of their own, getting royalties out of these guys was an act of oral surgery. "Have you ever actually seen royalty statements from some of these outfits? No one has. Hollywood could learn from these characters."

"You have no fucking idea what you're talking about. You're just talking to hear yourself talk."

And so on, to and fro, each party giving, I believe, as good as he or she got.

Barkerville was unseasonably chilly in the sense that Cynthia could not stand to speak to me or even look at me any more, but kept her distance as we pretended to enjoy the heritage buildings from the log church at the beginning of the High Street to the tiny stretch of resurrected Chinatown at the end. I can still see her trudging along the footpaths with her hands in her pockets and never taking her eyes from her feet. If I'd been closer I'm sure I could have heard her muttering and cursing. For my part, I felt terrible, absolutely drained and horrified, yet I felt relieved as well, even renewed.

I knew if we kept going our separate ways, weaving among the broken-down buckboards and sleighs in weedy lots next to stables and other out-buildings, we'd meet up again. We did, and her tone was calm; she had collected herself.

"They're trying to keep this from being just a museum," she said. "They're trying to put some life in it with the Chinese restaurant and the Chinese store up there. Real businesses. I'm sure there'll be more of this. The latest one is the hotel." This is a genuine mid-Victorian hotel midway up the principal street. "People can actually get a room there now and spend the night." I hadn't known this. "So that's what I think you should do. I'm going back by myself."

"You're leaving me in Barkerville?"

"You'll be fine."

And I was. I was feeling hurt and hollow now that the argument had ended, but if I'm honest with myself I admit I was feeling slightly exhilarated as well. We'd exchanged more than a sharp word or two. This was a genuine confrontation, the one I'd never had with Faye. I was quite getting into the BC history stuff. I read all the interpretive material and decided to hike up Williams Creek where the gold claims were, to be alone and think. Moving at my own pace, I walked an hour perhaps and then went over in the direction of places named Antler Creek and Yank's Peak, and kept coming upon old campsites: not historical ones, modern ones that were old enough to be dead. I experienced a good deal of discomfort in the left side of my chest after a while, but when I stopped, the feeling stopped also. So I went back to the hotel room—tiny, wallpapered, big brass bed, totally believable—and worried.

As it happened, the hotel was managed by the same German couple who owned the one in Wells. By telling them how much I enjoyed both establishments, I ingratiated myself enough to beg a ride to Quesnel, the nearest place of substance, with their employee who was going there to do the week's shopping. It seemed less unattractive than Williams Lake, less mallish, less ugly architecturally, but hot. Fearing what I was doing to my already overburdened credit card, I flew back to Vancouver and checked into the Sylvia Hotel, a place I had often passed and had heard about. There I waited for just a bit more time to elapse before attempting to effect a reconciliation with Cynthia. I killed hours walking along the Seawall, and I had no chest difficulties whatever, probably because I was, once again, on a level surface. There was just enough sea breeze to take the edge off the heat but nothing to obscure the sun. The path was crowded with strollers, joggers, runners, cyclists and rollerbladers, and people from Japan taking pictures of one another excitedly, repeatedly. A few minutes into the walk I saw the most extraordinarily beautiful African-Canadian woman in the most miniature red bikini. The contrast between it and her beautiful skin the colour of Belgian chocolate was quite a sight, and she had attracted a small crowd of admirers trying to give the impression they were not looking at her when they were, while her own air of indifference bore rather more conviction.

A bit farther along, at Second Beach, I stopped to watch a retriever puppy, not too many weeks out of the basket with its siblings crawling over one another, as it made what I thought might be its first water-borne retrieval, a contest between instinct on the one paw and common sense on the other: I know I'm supposed to fetch this stick but good grief that surf's bigger than I am. I watched a sea bird trying to take off with its beak full of a starfish the exact colour of grape Kool-Aid and another one dropping a mussel on the concrete from a great height to crack it open. I overheard wonderful snippets of conversation from people whizzing past on rollerblades, the sort of fragments I have since been collecting. The best was a lad casually saying to his mate: "If I won the lottery, I'd get a blowjob every day at breakfast." No one could write material like that. I was feeling more relaxed than I had been the past little while and so perhaps that is what made me feel a bit more optimistic as well—optimistic as well as lucky. The next morning, walking near the hotel, I saw one of those street-corner clinics they have more of in Vancouver than in other cities I know. I was one of the first patients of the day and got to see a doctor without a long wait. I detailed the symptoms, the trouble I had been having and under what circumstances. I told her about the amount of stress in my life, hoping, still naïvely, that this might suggest a line of diagnosis related to it. "If I were you, I would have a full set of tests for my heart." She was talking about angina, but I asked how that could be when I didn't have pain as such, only discomfort and loss of breath sometimes—not always when I was doing something strenuous, in fact usually not. "There's no single set of symptoms that applies in all cases. I think you need a stress test. It's a very simple test, done on a treadmill. Depending on the results, other procedures might be called for. I see you don't live in BC."

"No, I'm only visiting, but I'm here fairly often."

"I think you should see your own physician when you return to Ontario, if you're planning to be back there soon."

I was shocked in the sense that all the soul-saving rationalisations with which I'd been keeping my spirit alive seemed to fall away beneath my feet like the trap door of the gallows. My plans for the future were already beginning to go a bit spongy. Now I had reason to question the most basic hope on which anybody's future plans depend. I rushed to phone Cynthia. She answered coolly but sensed the importance of what I had to tell her. She told me to come over but I asked if she could come to the hotel. I don't know, I suppose I thought neutral ground, on which we had no history together, would be better, though this is said with purifying hindsight. In truth, I wasn't thinking logically. In the face of such news, we made up quickly. Perhaps we would have done so anyway. She said that in January she would move to Toronto whether she had a job or not. I didn't hear the conviction in her voice I was hoping to pick up, but then this may well have been some problem with my receiver rather than her transmitter. Or was I still playing mind games with myself? By nature I am a pessimistic person (though I might say *realistic* and others might say *cynical*). At least I was when I had no reason to be terrified. Was I now clinging to more optimism than I was entitled to by rights? She stayed the night even though she didn't have anything to sleep in or a toothbrush or anything and was sure to have a ticket on her windscreen in the morning.

As soon as I recovered from the effects of the red-eye back to Toronto, I phoned my doctor but I got only his answering service and he never returned the call. Then to my alarm, his number simply went out of service. We have all read stories about the decline in

health care, but were family doctors having their phones discon-
nected? As my shrink had once fired me, so now I fired my MD,
except that I couldn't get in touch with him to give him the news.
So I called the College of Physicians and Surgeons where I was direct-
ed to the website where they list doctors who are accepting new
patients. I found one downtown, amazingly, and got an appointment
only ten days hence. Despite Pam's best efforts, the office was an
absolute shambles of people angry with me for not getting back to
them as I apparently had been promising to do for months. I suddenly wondered if my old doctor hadn't been having a meltdown.
That I could sympathize with.

The time until this point I remember in quite clear detail. From
here onward, however, everything becomes, no not a blur but rather
a sort of running together of blotches and elements in a way that is
almost psychedelic. I got to see the doctor, a confident young woman
who instils confidence in others by being so. She booked my stress
test, ordered up blood work and, at my suggestion, had the lab count
my sperm (which came back eighty-eight per cent, "very good for
a man your age," which appeared to please Cynthia when I relayed
the results).

Autumn was upon us now and there was talk of an Air Canada
strike that everyone was trying to beat, which thus made Canadian
Airlines equally impossible. Cynthia queued up for standby on four
successive flights and managed to get a seat. What a joy to see her
again. We had a wonderful few days. We had fun, talked seriously,
deepened our whole relationship or so I thought at the time, and
made love on all her three most fertile days, though I was able to
perform adequately on only the first and third and then with considerable effort; on the other I could not summon the energy, seemed not

have enough oxygen; Cynthia was understanding. We went to the big annual McClelland and Stewart party at the AGO where I heard a rumour circulated by Bob Mulligan that Cynthia and I were getting married now that my divorce was final. The second part was true enough, but I tried to scotch the first part, and debated whether to tell Cynthia who was somewhere on the far side of the room. She pretended to take it well enough when I decided I should tell her because she would learn of it soon enough anyway. By the same logic, I called Faye the next day—our first contact in a while—and was relieved to find her in a reasonable mood. So I again brought up the subject of Cynthia and reminded her gently that she had no reason to be uncivil to her when she came here to live, bygones being bygones and inasmuch as our marriage had always been troubled, perhaps even doomed. I expected a blow-up but Faye agreed. She said, "I wish you would live in Vancouver," making it sound more like an order than a suggestion. When Cynthia went back this time, it felt like winter. Not literally, thank God, as the motor on the furnace had burned out and needed replacing with money I wasn't sure I had (my accounts were an absolute thicket now). I considered finding a roommate to help share expenses, but didn't know anyone. Pam offered to put the word out. She also offered to try to sort out my GST. Revenue Canada was threatening to turn my case over to legal branch.

Cynthia and I decided that she would come to Toronto in October and I'd go to Vancouver in November, but by now I was beginning to wonder if or to what extent she was continuing the relationship because I was ill with what still could not, it seemed, be diagnosed successfully. To the extent she was offering to take care of me, was this a rechannelling (or a perversion) of the maternal feeling she had discovered in herself? Why did I worry so? I resolved simply to take her at her word, and her latest word was still that she was moving to Toronto sometime in January, more than a year after my return from Europe when life started to collapse around me like a wobbly bridge table. She was like me, like the rest of us: slowly being abraded and eroded by daily living but a bloody marvel in those special moments of communication. We had one such shortly afterwards, a long tender call, full of ideas and understanding. I told her for the first time how ambivalent, not to say resentful, I was about my Jewishness when I was a teenager but had grown into it, you might say—grown out of my failure to embrace it—in time to experience the pleasure of my parents' relief.

"Have you ever been the victim of anti-Semitism?"

I was touched by the question's simplicity. I needed a moment to find an answer, any answer.

"Not about the important stuff." One of those bumpy pauses I dislike. "A lot of people don't understand and most of them are too awkward or uncomfortable to ask." I could tell by listening to how she listened that I had said the right thing in the right way. I heard her apprehension vanish like air going out of a tyre. The satisfaction from an exchange like that lasts much longer than what we used to get from phone sex in the first months of the relationship.

We still found humour in each other as well. Much of our time on the phone was taken up with telling the other one about our days. This is a major reason the LDR worked as well as it did. Simply by hearing about them so much, I felt I was getting to know the friends of hers I had never met and perhaps getting sympathy for the ones who'd been at her birthday party.

I told her about being at Greg Gatenby's annual Harbourfront party and bumping into Eleanor Sims who surprised me by insisting we go to dinner the following week. I was surprised even more when she rang the very next day to establish the exact date. I have always liked her company and was resigned to the fact that she had never apologised to a social inferior (this is what I mean by anti-Semitism but never about anything terribly important). So I was looking forward to a relaxing dinner when I picked her up at her new place, where she had settled after her divorce. As I told Cynthia, she did a curious thing. When I arrived at seven-thirty I heard her tell her teenager that she would be home at ten. It was a very casual evening; she was in a sweater and slacks with no discernible make-up. But at nine forty-five, after the bill had come and she had insisted on carefully splitting it, she went to the ladies' and emerged heavily rouged, mascara'd and lipstuck. I asked Cynthia to explain what this meant, and she howled. "I'm the last person who'd know that! I know a lot of people out here who wear lipstick but all of them are men, or used to be."

I told her I thought I was being used as a beard. I was surprised, because it's customary to ask the beard's permission first.

❋ ❋ ❋

When things really began to go to hell, they did so quickly, but though the velocity increased, there was never an end in sight. When she came in October, Cynthia was distant to say the least. The first night she woke me to complain that I was snoring (Faye had never told me I snored and to say the least it is the sort of thing she would have mentioned eternally). Later I felt her climbing out of bed; I could hear her anger in the dark though she said nothing as she took covers and trudged noisily off to the sofa. I confronted her in the morning and she said she had been having nightmares. The next night too we slept apart, but on the third I got a more satisfactory answer. Not a full one, of course, nor the only, but plausible and perfectly understandable as far as it went.

"I don't like sleeping in the bed you slept in with Faye."

"All right. Easily dealt with. But it never bothered you before."

"Well, it does now."

"I'll take care of it. We'll go shopping for one you like."

She now had the look of someone who was about to snarl.

The visit was short but the rest of it followed those lines. Once she had gone, I tried to move the bed down the stairs and out to the kerb, but I didn't seem to have the strength, or the knowledge. I remembered it now: Faye and I had started out with an Ikea bed but then we had this one custom made by some carpenter acquaintance of hers so that there were big drawers for blankets and sheets built into it and bookcases in the headboard (wildly impractical of course). I couldn't figure out how to take it apart, then remembered that it had been constructed in the room, not brought in whole. There were some tools in the cellar, and I got the saw and began to dissect the damn thing, but that would be an immense task, practically a career. I knew what to do. I went to Canadian Tire at Yonge and Davenport and bought an electric saw. They showed me what they called a Skilsaw but it looked too dangerous for an amateur who lacked the requisite Skil. The clerk asked what I needed it for, but saying I had to cut the marital bed into pieces to save the relationship with my girlfriend sounded absurd (especially the word *girlfriend*). He sold me what he called a jigsaw. This did the trick, though it took a long while and the pieces I hauled puffing out to the street where bigger than I would have liked. I rebuked myself for being in possession of such thoughts. At this stage in my autobiographical melodrama did I really give a fuck what the neighbours might think of such unavoidable symbolism?

Vancouver the next month was worse. On her three most fertile days we didn't have sex. Nor on the days either side. The Monday, which she was to take off work, she spent at the office anyway, and when she came home she threw a temper tantrum because I was too exhausted to go to her yoga class with her. Evidently she was studying not tantric yoga but tantrum yoga. Later I learned that yoga rage is a social problem peculiar to Vancouver, but at the time I was ignorant of local matters.

"How can you be exhausted?" she said. "You haven't done anything."

But I was too tired to defend myself, so she carried on with anger enough for both of us. Finally I could stand it no longer and offered to go elsewhere. She refused to hear of it. But she wouldn't calm down. In the end, I threw all my things in my bag and decamped for the Sylvia in a heavy rain without saying where I was going. Rain like that could be classified as assault. That and other factors kept me in the room the next morning except when I went out looking for a book or some magazines to buy. A Chinese newsagent chased me out of her hole-in-the-wall shop for reading, screaming that reading is costing her "thousands of dollars a week". I sat on a wet bench, one of the ones with little plaques that memorialise friends and relatives who have died, particularly in the great stress and depression epidemics, I believe; I checked the tide's respiration. When I got back there was a message from Cynthia. She knew I would be in the West End at the Sylvia, of course. She was as smart as Faye. But the message wasn't really from her; she was simply passing on one from Pam about crises at the office. For Pam not to be able to solve such problems herself was unusual, but why did she think I could do any better in my present state? I didn't ignore it. I simply didn't do anything about it.

After twenty-four hours or so of soothing self-pity, I gave up and phoned Cynthia. She was still furious, saying she would come to Toronto but wouldn't be living with me. My stress, she said contemptuously, was of no concern to her. She also said: "We have different values."

I tried to sound light-hearted when I replied: "I imagine mine are the wrong ones."

I've often thought about her other-values line the past few years. I have never been able to determine if she meant that I'm Jewish or that she isn't. The interpretation depends on my state. I remember the one time, during the Wells-Barkerville argument, when she made such a point of my not being as Canadian as she is. I should have said: "You were conscripted, I volunteered." It was not that I wasn't quick enough to do so, it was a case rather of neither of us being able to communicate with the other—in my case, I suppose, for fear of what worse things I might find: something anti-Semitic, I realise now, is perhaps what I feared deep down, some epithet that would ruin my record as a recipient of tolerance and test my reputation as a purveyor of it.

What hurt, of course, was that, suddenly and without saying a word, she was finished with trying to get pregnant. The façade cracked in Toronto, just as it had with Faye years ago, but this time the shards fell in Vancouver. Once this was established, I continued to feel betrayed, as the weak do, and she probably went on being angry, for the selfish remain that way when they cannot manipulate those closest to them to their own complete satisfaction.

I seemed to be staying a long time in the city where I didn't feel wanted any longer. I wasn't sure what I thought might happen. I surprised myself by sleeping well that night, as though totally exhausted from a day in a logging camp. I surprised myself even more by getting up at seven-thirty the next morning and walking two and a half hours round the Seawall in rain of tropical force—with no shortness of breath whatever. Possibly the two events are connected, I thought. I was hoping this was about the womb-twitches having let up suddenly and lack of commitment to commitment itself, not about anything as mundane as jobs. I thought: How bizarre. The women's magazine stereotypes are utterly reversed. I am the one who wanted to talk about the relationship, she's the one who couldn't handle her feelings. You could never sell this as a script except possibly as an episode of some especially dreadful sitcom.

The next morning I was hurrying to make check-out time when she phoned and asked to come over. She stayed less than two hours during which time we had a long emotionally charged round-robin. She broke the news I already knew. Our relationship? "There is no relationship." Thinking back now, I know none of this could have been easy for her, for the situation itself came wrapped in implied self-criticism. At least this was one turning point we weren't experiencing over the phone.

✻ ✻ ✻

To make a long story somewhat more compact, I continued to have what I was told were low-level symptoms of—what? One set of doctors thought it was a muscular/skeletal problem. Others feared it was my bronchial tree. Another suspected the liver was to blame. But in fact they were all mistaken. I did not have skeletal, lung, heart or liver anything. I had cancer, a type I had never heard of, called oat cell carcinoma. There was a tumour in my left lung, in the right apical lobe (I know all this terminology now). That of course was the bad news. The good news, at least by comparison, was that the cancer was localised in just the one place. *In situ.* That's what saved me. Still, any treatment had better be done sooner rather than later, and the oncologist was certain he could effect a surgical cure instead of treating it with radiation.

I debated whether to tell Cynthia I was to go under the knife, to use an old expression of my father's. I could play the stoic and keep silent, letting her learn the news by the publishing grapevine, or I could risk rebuke. I decided to leave her a message at home when I knew she would be at work. I was to be admitted to hospital, I would say. I tried to script the call mentally beforehand, so as not to ramble or sound maudlin. But I'm sure there was fear in my voice that a few weak jokes failed to disguise, and though I thought I was being orderly and concise, I used up all the time allowed for message-leaving on her old-fashioned machine and had to call a second time with the last part. I couldn't imagine how she would receive all of this.

❋ ❋ ❋

I write this in Vancouver on a typical winter's morning. The forecast calls for scattered showers turning to bronchitis by late afternoon. One morning last week we had our snowfall. A couple of centimetres of non-sticky stuff appeared, trolley buses stopped running and schools were closed. The mayor appeared on television to appeal for calm. Then troops were called in to shoot looters. It happens every other year. In this atmosphere, I try to remember what it was like back east. I was in hospital rather less than a week. When I awoke in the ICU, a nurse told me that Cynthia from Vancouver had called to ask about my condition. There was no other message. I was most of a year recovering my full strength. I never got round to getting another bed but slept on the mattress on the floor, like a seventies commune-dweller. I thought constantly about life and death. I had survived but as people kept telling me, needlessly, my life would never be the same; I had the mark on me and must learn to live for however long I was to live. However well mended, a thing once diseased is never so strong as it was. I thought a great deal about messes as well. In publishing there are many of them, but I'm thinking more about the non-professional ones. Many are trivial, though some are profound; some are deactivated by the passage of time, a few solved but many others merely lie dormant, the file never actually closed. Our messes mutate and ultimately define us. Mine do.

And I thought about what I should be doing with the rest of my life. In the first two months or more after surgery, Pam did a great deal of taking care of me. I was pretty much broke after paying Faye for her half of the house, and the agency was nearly ruined. Pam could save it but only if she had the authority. So I decided to give it to her, the works, asking for only a share of the profits (I don't expect any) for the first five years. But she would have to move the business to a proper office somewhere, because I was going to sell the house, fast and cheaply, retire the mortgage and move to Vancouver with the difference. After years spent giving advice to writers while secretly wanting to be on the other side of the desk, I knew that now was the time. I needed a new place to live this new life, and I had become attached to Vancouver and fancied I had come to understand something important about it. Vancouver runneth over with writers but this is precisely because it has no readers to speak of.

Reading in a kayak is difficult and dangerous, so Vancouverites by and large avoid it. Since the big Duthie's went out of business, it doesn't even have any bookshops worthy of the name except for a few small struggling independents in farflung neighbourhoods, remote from downtown. A perfect place to work, away from validating distractions yet alive with professional companionship and a certain productive poverty (Vancouver writers have all been lending one another the same fifty dollars for years now—for so long that the banknote has King George on it—George V, not even VI). Of course, a move like that is fraught with complications and qualifications. My parents, for example. But they were still in good health and among their friends; they would be less content on the West Coast where, among other things, the Jewish community, not to say the European community, is less obvious than in Central Canada.

Having made so many messes in my life, I find great satisfaction in being able to fix one or to see one seem to fix itself as passions heal. Not long before I came west, I actually ran into Faye outside the supermarket on Dupont and persuaded her, with effort, to have a quick coffee. "I was sorry to hear you were ill," she said with what she couldn't fool me into believing was other than sincerity as far as it went, however understated, however galling it might be to have to say it out loud. When I phoned Cynthia to tell her of my decision, however, she flared up, accusing me of moving to BC because I was hoping to win her back—stalking her almost. She moved from her old place in Kits to somewhere on the East Side, I don't know where precisely, though I could have learned the address easily enough. I expected that I would catch glimpses of her on occasions such as the BC Book Prizes or the International Writers' Festival party. As I imagined the scene, she would slowly grow quite civil, if briskly and efficiently so. I kept thinking that this would make a good story. It's not a Greek tragedy. No one dies at the end. It's a Canadian tragedy. Everybody feels bad and blames someone else.

II

I had not lived alone for a very long time if you don't count (and I do not) living alone in the emotional sense during the latter years of the marriage. Nor do I count the LDR, because when Cynthia and I were together we were cohabitating intermittently, so to speak. Or so I prefer to think of it, though no doubt that is being foolish. Therefore I was in a seldom visited state of mind when I resettled in the West End and moved into this tidy and tiny one-bedroom apartment, still not having quite accommodated myself to *suite*.

Whenever I must leave the West End, with its thick forest of off-white and pastel high-rises, all of them different, it is only to walk downtown where existence wears more layers. You still see many buildings carried forward from the boom that the Great War brought to an end: the office buildings with brass mail chutes and marble floors or the squat four-storey hotels with enormous windows that in summer swing open on pivots, like weather vanes moving with the wind. Both are run down. The office blocks seemed to be filled with fly-by-night language schools and Chinese import-export businesses, the hotels with retired loggers and fishermen, here known as *fishers*. Everything else is brand new. Then, after dark, the mean age drops by half and the place looks and sounds like the set of *Blade Runner*. The difference between day and night is literally the difference between day and night.

These are the two neighbourhoods I know and where I feel surprisingly comfortable. The others I avoid. Even now, Kitsilano reminds me of Cynthia, the loss of Cynthia, and I stare across English Bay at its defiant leafiness when I'm strolling on the Seawall. It is like foreign territory that I once was familiar with, long ago, before the war you might say, but has no doubt changed beyond all recognition now, making my recollections worthless. Out on my walks, I see the North Shore as well, with North Van and West Van slowly slipping up the mountains in defiance of gravity, and I sometimes wonder what it would be like to board the ferry that keeps moving silently across the harbour and across the shipping lane between the downtown waterfront and Lonsdale Quay. The West Side I pass through rarely and by taxi; East Vancouver is an abstraction with which I do not correspond. Yes, my map has shrunk quite a bit, but I keep telling myself that I live more deeply now.

Talking with my parents on the phone every week, I began to realise all that they have known without telling me, things I was just now coming to understand, even at my age. The benefit of exile is one of these. One night I woke with the sudden understanding that exile often leads to a higher state of awareness (forgive me if I sound like a Kitsilano Buddhist)—*higher* of course meaning *deeper*. Another night not long afterwards I lay awake thinking for some reason about monks and hermits. The mind often works most quickly when the body is exhausted, and my body runs out of fuel easily these days. In this state I suddenly experienced some sort of synaptic leap: "Being an exile is much like being a contemplative hermit. Same status in the majority society, which takes one's existence as an unvoiced criticism of itself, which perhaps it actually is. I got up and turned on my new computer, which I was only beginning to learn how to use for anything more complicated than email, and found myself thinking, as I did many times every day and especially each evening, of Cynthia, wondering what different life she herself was leading outside work (that is to say, leading with whom, if anyone). Such questions always brought me back to the larger essential one. Not why did she leave me. Not why did she put an end to the relationship. But what was the source or at least the nature of the communications breakdown that, it seems to me, was more in the nature of a cause than an effect.

I was supposed to be taking care to get enough rest at night and to exercise during the day. Sometimes I became frightened to realise how very freely I was interpreting doctor's orders. But on such evenings I found I had opened a sally port to the recent past, that I had total recall. Perhaps this is what dying people, or those who believe they are dying whether slowly or quickly, always experience. Your life flashes before your eyes, as the cliché has it. In my case, it was not flashing but rather returning to me ever so slowly and in agonising detail and in a way that was evidently self-perpetuating. The man who is his own therapist has a fool for a patient: that may well be. But I found myself replaying every moment of those months with Cynthia. I did so partly because I *could* do so. The more I thought about her, the more of our old conversations came back to me, in such exacting detail as to be of almost stenographic completeness.

Amazing. When we were together, she had mesmerised me. Now her memory seemed able to hypnotise me by means of some remote connection, a wireless mind-modem of some type, I am not certain what to call it as I'm not at all sure I know what I am talking about. Yet I know what was happening to me.

I would try to put the memory fragments into categories, always creating new files. "Do you wish to save or delete? Save. Save as? Everything Cynthia ever said about sex." That might provide some explanation or at least a clue, I hoped.

Sex made her happy. Big surprise. When I was at the top of my game and we were clicking, she would climax with a thunderous report, with such moaning as would seem false were it in a movie, but never with actual speech. Fortunately, she always climaxed before I did, though of course this was probably a statement on my age and condition, not some tantric practice I have mastered, the sort taught in seminars I always see advertised in the *Georgia Straight*. But while I had no delusions about excessive masculine vigour, I would, during her subsequent subverbal outbursts, think to myself that I had done well for someone whom long years of marriage had provided a decreasing number of opportunities to perfect whatever technique I had. She knew how to cum even if she did not know how to kiss. But sex made her cross as well.

We didn't know it—I didn't know it—at the time, but my body was giving way under the slow undermining force of the oat cell. Although I was still able to perform as required, I did need quite a bit of assistance at the beginning, a fact I had put down to aging, which is doubtless partly what it was as well and not merely a symptom. Cynthia didn't always care for oral sex, receiving or giving. I didn't take this personally, presuming that the receiving spoke to some sensitivity on her part in excess of what a person would consider normal pleasure. I asked her about this once in a particularly open and candid exchange, believing such questions can be softly put, but she cut me off, then covered her retreat with more of her inexplicably awful kisses. As to her aversion to giving rather than receiving head, I understood it suddenly on my birthday. She asked me with her naughtiest diagonal leer what kind of sex I wanted as a present. Not wishing to seem gauche as well as louche, I replied that a thorough sucking of the cock might do the job nicely. We were in bed at the time though dressed, but she unbuttoned the white top she was wearing and unhooked her bra, letting her breasts swing freely as she bent down to take my penis between her lips. I thought: "Well she's certainly entering into the spirit of the occasion. Maybe we can do more of this. Maybe all she needed was the right partner?"

She had one hand playing with my testicles like Captain Queeg at his court martial in *The Caine Mutiny* fiddling obsessively with those ball bearings. Her other hand was stroking the base of the cock shaft while her mouth came up and down on the upper portion. Now I was the one moaning so loudly as to wake her neighbours. She withdrew her mouth just before I ejaculated but kept using her hand on my bollocks. Suddenly she called out, sharply enough to make me open my eyes with a start. "Shit!" she said. She seemed to be looking at her open blouse fluttering either side of her torso. At first I thought I'd messed it by shooting off. Then I saw the red blots. Dear God, I've got blood in my sperm! Then I saw that, no, she was having a nosebleed. She jumped up and got the box of tissue on the night table while whipping off the blouse and running to the bathroom to turn on the tap.

"Are you all right?"

"I get nosebleeds when I'm too tense having sex," she said, as though this were somehow my fault.

"That's awful," I said sympathetically as well as with surprise, no astonishment. "You poor thing. This is upsetting."

"Why?" she shot back angrily. "Does it remind you of menstrual blood?"

There seemed to be no possible response to that beyond a simple "No, of course not." She was soaking the blouse in the basin as I watched, amazed at her way of ending a conversation with the face-to-face equivalent of concluding a telephone conversation by slamming the receiver in the caller's ear.

She was angry for about an hour, long after she had changed her blouse for a sweatshirt. Perhaps longer, for at that stage she told me she wanted to be alone. I didn't know whether she wished me to leave or was planning to go out herself. I fumbled a bit and in a few minutes she was in her coat going through the door. I tried to read but couldn't concentrate. I myself didn't wish to leave lest she telephoned while I was out. She returned at dinner time, the clouds having passed overhead or at least been tucked out of the way.

"Here. Happy birthday." She had hired three videos. "I asked what Jewish films they had and they just looked at me funny and mentioned *Fiddler on the Roof*, but I figure you hate musicals as much as I do. So I went English instead."

There was an early Hitchcock I don't think I had ever seen, *Hard Day's Night* which I hadn't watched for years actually, and of all things a Benny Hill compilation. She perhaps saw my eyebrows rise a bit as I saw the last of these, which claimed to be "the best", a highly provocative assertion.

"Guys like these, right? Girls losing their skirts and all that."

I was touched in a way but I forget what I muttered in response before asking her if she would like to watch the young Beatles with me.

She was a plain-spoken, conversation-stopping young woman all right. Once we were talking about Canada and the idea of immigration and deracination. I quoted Robert Frost's definition of home as that place where, when you have to go there, they must take you in. "You have that, you see, but I don't," I said.

"I thought that's what Israel's for."

Which was not really what I had been thinking of at all. In her own way, however, she did have a talent for cutting through to the heart of the matter, even if only by suddenly putting an end to all conversation, one way or another.

She was proud of her breasts, with good reason, I thought. They were high round discs, quite large in circumference but not especially protuberant, not in a way that would attract crude remarks or even envy, at least not among people, the lucky few (or many—I didn't know and didn't care; it was none of my concern really) who had had the pleasure of seeing them in their uncovered state. They were the perfect secret breasts, looking so ordinary when hidden by a coating or two of clothing. In deference to what she must have considered a kind of conversational etiquette—a strange concept to ascribe to her of all people; maybe it was as much a conceit as a social nicety—she felt obliged to denigrate them.

"They're really not that big."

I believe I smiled. "Women always believe their breasts are too small, or, in certain cases, too large. The truth is they're always perfect just as they are to the men who care about them."

I thought that was a rather tactful statement if I say so myself. It also had the additional benefit of being, in my own observation and experience, true. How could she possibly mistake my tone? But she did.

"I suppose this is some kind of trade-off. You're saying women should be the same way about cocks."

"Many probably are, I suppose. But I'm not so well informed on that side of things." I was careful in how I made this sound, and this seemed to blunt her sharp edges in that instance.

I've always believed that sex is the purest form of communication between individuals. It is communication unimpeded by words. It makes talk unnecessary. I say this even though I am obviously a person driven by language in the other departments of life, whereas Cynthia, though just as obviously not a word person (she thought publishing a minor branch of show business), managed to make a mess of it. She missed signals from others, sent out false positives by the bundle, fostered misunderstandings right and left. Of course, the cumulative effect of all this wasn't apparent to me at the time. Now of course it is, especially late at night when after a long session in front of the screen I retire to bed and lie there reliving every moment in a way that could be called Proustian if it were not so nightmarish. Then I finally take off my glasses, fold them neatly on the night table and call in some of the debt that sleep owes us— only to find myself awake again in three or four hours, when I must take a sleeping pill, knowing that I will start off the next day with a foggy hangover without, sadly, having passed through the normal stage of bacchanalian overindulgence or indeed had any fun at all. In these moments, the story keeps coming back to me, like a guest who refuses to go home, not that you truly wish him gone, however much he disrupts your routine simply by his presence—his existence really.

At such times, I often think of how in a sense our roles seemed reversed. I was the one who had been married for so long and had little information about, how would you say, *contemporary* scxual practices. She was the savvy single person, young(er) or youngish, actively dating (I sound so old-fashioned—I mean fucking), going to clubs. You would expect her to be different, more forthcoming, while to my surprise I have become a professional eroticist since she shut me out of her life. Who could have foreseen that?

I remember when the process began. It was shortly after the day when she was in such a light-hearted mood and started to tell me about searching for pornographic stories on Google. Later, the subject came up again, also playfully, and resulted in some glancing remarks, leading remarks, about sexual fantasies. What were mine?

I had to ponder that for a moment.

"I imagine they're the usual ones," I said. "Having sex with two women at the same time. Then watching politely while they carry on themselves."

"That's what I figured. I knew your fantasy life would be a cliché." She said this, however, with a smile in her voice.

"I suppose yours defies categorisation."

"No, I wouldn't say that." She was serious now, a rare moment devoid of either laughter or brittleness. "You can probably guess mine too."

I said that I couldn't possibly.

"Oh you know. I've always wanted—always wondered what it would be like to be blacked."

This must have registered on my face. I wasn't familiar with the verb except in the sense of boots being blackened or, in older times, stoves and stovepipes. She looked slightly peeved and just a tiny bit embarrassed.

"You know, I want to be fucked by a black man."

This was followed by the scurrying sound subjects make when they are suddenly being changed. But I began thinking about this brief exchange almost at once. How difficult could it possibly be in cities like Toronto or Vancouver to find a randy man of African descent? And how complicated she was beneath her dislike of irony, or her lack of it—a kind of communicative anaemia: irony deficiency. I've thought about this exchange a great deal more since then. I remember that the thought even galloped across my mind when I was in hospital, recovering. You might suppose anything even slightly erotic would have been the farthest thing from my mind. Certainly I was in no condition to act on any such impulse, no condition even to concentrate. I suppose when life is suddenly uncertain, tenuous, the brain keeps flitting, unsuccessfully, to other topics to distract itself from the dread and fear, if only for a few seconds at a time. I suppose this is why patients who are dying so often seem to be speaking stream-of-consciousness fashion. Or maybe it is the medication in their bloodstreams combining with the taste of death newly on their tongues. In any case, *blacked* is another of the keywords that even then recurred in my personal twilight as I lay in bed at night trying to keep the damn screen from flashing images at me one after another. Other times, stretched out beneath the blankets on my mattress on the floor, I wondered if when she was fucking other men she was using birth control. Why had I never seen any evidence? Why had she never asked me to use a condom before we decided to have a child? Why had the subject never even come up? I was still in a sort of shock realising that she hadn't really wanted to have a child with me, that I just happened to be the person who was handy when the urge struck. She wanted excitement but not with me, just as she wanted a baby but not, she decided, mine. But no, I don't know any of this for certain. All I know is that there was brief but intense passion that existed in our time en route to being a memory.

She was after all another Protestant. Lack of communication was part of their culture. Jews can't stop communicating with one another. Every seder I have attended in my parents' home has been a pious cacophony of attempted communication with one another as well as with thousands of years of tradition. No two people ever seemed to be reading from the same edition of the book, probably never even from the same translation. One person's page seven was the next person's page nine. Communication was unrestrained if noisy and messy. WASPs are different, and Canadian ones especially, I sometimes think. It is a schoolbook truism that Canadians, being so few people set down on such a giant piece of real estate, have excelled at inventions related to communicating over great distances. The telephone of course, the radio vacuum tube, the wire photo, the ATM, the software that I believe is now used on stock exchanges round the world. But such machines and devices are really so many intermediaries between individuals and groups, making it less and less necessary for the people to have true conversations with one another, to read one another's faces as they absorb the words being spoken. They have made their weakness into some sort of faux Buddhist virtue: the communication of non-communication. You would not expect such a concept to come between Cynthia and me in the early part of our LDR, for indeed even Faye and I had mutual understanding going for us once upon a time, strange as that now seems when her non-communicativeness too has altered me in fundamental ways, to the point where I wouldn't know honestly what to say to her if she were in fact speaking to me. But it was at precisely such moments of optimal potential that Cynthia sabotaged empathy and voice. The situation in which her feelings might have flowed freely instead seemed to piss her off. She was constantly on the verge of being offended. I didn't know why and neither did she. But I've known this fact all along: the truly interesting people are always very complicated. One must relish their complexity or give up on them.

✳ ✳ ✳

I resettled here in early spring just as the shopkeepers along Denman Street began putting out water bowls for the dogs that in good weather constantly parade their masters and mistresses up and down the pavement. I was "recovering" but recovering from what and to what extent? My body had been invaded and a piece of it removed as plunder. Thus had my life been saved. There had been a rebellion and I had been given a death sentence and then a reprieve, not a pardon but a reprieve, one that could be rescinded at any time. In effect, I had been autopsied while still alive. The loss of appetite, the weight loss, these were shorthand references to a greater loss—of reasonable certainty, of the magisterial assumption that there would always be a future up ahead. There was now a dividing line running down the centre of my existence. On one side of it were all the years when I never paid the slightest mind to what was going on inside my chest. On the other side, nothing in there would ever feel right again. If in moments of distraction, which I sought out more and more on my solitary computer screen, I sometimes succeeded in putting the changes out of my mind, my attention was quickly and forcibly returned to the agenda by the realisation that I now lacked the breath for some relatively minor exertions. We all reach the summit beyond which there is only a decline. Illness is like religion: something higher than oneself. Now my life was about death. As some time passed, I could not recall what being healthy ever felt like. I actually knew in real time that I had begun the descent. In these periods I found great comfort, far more so than I would have imagined, in talking to my father.

I suppose I had felt guilty about moving west when they were the age they were, but as I said to myself, "At least they have each other," and that was true enough as far as it went. I don't believe I was rationalising away any unpleasant truths when I added that they were comfortable in their own home in North Toronto in the circle of friends they had been part of for so long, though the ranks were beginning to thin somewhat. For his part, Father felt guilty that I was spending so much money phoning him twice a week.

"Not to worry. I've signed up with Sprint. This costs only pennies a minute. Trust me. Really."

Was it because I didn't have anyone else in my life that I was paying more attention to such family as I had? I remembered what I had said to Cynthia about Robert Frost but didn't understand quite correctly back then: home was not a place after all but the family and, yes, they would have had to take me back if I had asked. Yet it was the disconnectedness I was nevertheless feeling that seemed always to become the topic of these calls (for, really, how much detail could I listen to about the people he and Mother played cards with, and how could I possibly tell him the sorts of things I was writing?— clearly I could not). So we talked about fitting in and not fitting in and seeming to fit in. The conversations always returned to this general topic. I think that my need to hear about the past coincided with his desire to talk about it. In one of these conversations I asked him a version of a question that Cynthia had once put to me: Did he really and honestly feel anti-Semitism had kept him from being what he wished to become? He answered more quickly and more decisively than I had expected.

"No, not here. Back there."

I pressed him for specifics, and this was where he paused thoughtfully, weighing his words, then weighing them a second time to be sure.

"I know where this is leading," he said. "Since you're my son, I'm supposed to give you the advice I think you're fishing for." Then his diction changed, as though he were quoting himself saying something he had perhaps often said but only in his head, never aloud. "With the Canadians", he said, "the thing is to always keep telling them how polite they are. If you forget for even a second, they'll throw a drink in your face."

I was so shocked I didn't know what to say. Nothing else anyone had said to me up until that time was so unexpected—not since Eleanor Sims called me an asshole. I could tell he was agitated, and the next time we talked I learned why.

"Your mother's not been well. She's been getting dizzy a great deal, her hands and feet are cold much of the time, and they can't figure out why."

"Circulatory." This was all I could think to say.

"Of course. But they've done various tests, all the normal ones. Many tests. Now they want her to stay in hospital a couple of days. We're hoping they'll get to the bottom of it, and that will be the end; they'll know how to treat whatever it is."

"I'm coming home."

"No, stay. Not to worry. Send her some nice flowers. But hurry, she'll be home before they arrive if you don't do it in the morning."

✳ ✳ ✳

If the nights can be difficult in this (and other) ways, the days can be unreal. I must get away from this computer screen and away from the apartment. I must use exercise to delay the inevitable, exercise being another of the things that is said to do the body good even if begun at the eleventh hour, like aspirin, vegetables and spiritual belief, though on the last of these opinion is divided.

I am the oldest person at the gym and evidently one of only a rather small quota of heteros. Twice a week I go to class. Monday's instructor does it deadpan. "Exercise the brain as you exercise the bod" is one of his exhortations. He is a thin young man whose blond hair is in triangular spikes, like the spines on the back of stegosaurus and perhaps other dinosaurs. "Don't use your glutes, use your abs!" is another stock utterance. I have actually heard him say, as though he were in a television series concerning California, "Do you feel the love? That's what we call the pain. The *love*."

Wednesday's instructor is one of the fittest young women I've ever seen or can imagine. In another and totally different respect she reminds me of myself, or rather of what I now see others sometimes found discomfiting about the old me, the pre-Cynthian me, the healthy me: the brassy and sometimes pathetic stand-up comedy with all its forced wordplay. One time she said: "There's a plumb line going down to the floor from your tail bone. An imaginary one, I hope." Another of her wisecracks: "Lift those shoulder blades off the mat. Don't just do elbow exercise. Momentum is your enemy.

And for some of you, so is Lycra!" This wasn't particularly well received by all members of the class. I understand she is an aspiring actress. A photo from her portfolio, quite glam, looking nothing whatever like her, hangs in the lobby, and occasionally she has to miss a class when it conflicts with an audition for a part she never gets.

The other days I walk the Seawall, going as quickly as I can for as far as I can for the sake of cardio and endurance, but the results are mixed at best. The landscape being the same, with only the moisture level varying from day to day, I try my best to keep it interesting. Sometimes I'll begin at First Beach and go clockwise, other times at Lost Lagoon and go counter-clockwise. Either way, I can manage a complete circumnavigation only rarely and after resting at the halfway point, somewhere near the Lions Gate Bridge. Eavesdropping on the conversations of other walkers and joggers, those not speaking in Japanese, is not merely another way of tricking the time into passing but also a way of putting onto others the burden of being funny, albeit unintentionally so in their case. If I am walking slowly, I will stop and write down a particularly meaty fragment. The cream of my collection is like the postcard fiction that enjoyed a short vogue in the early eighties, when I once sold an anthology of the stuff for a client, a friend of Blair's. Of my top seven, here are six:

- "Five hundred of 'em, all dressed in white. It was really something."
- "That's going to be worth six months' probation at least."
- "I said to him, 'My horoscope warned me about this.'"
- "And he turned out to be, like, a small-c Capricorn." (As God is my witness, I am not making this up.)

- "In my line of work, things like that don't happen."
- "I said what the fuck, and now she's yelling at me all the way to Safeway, right?"

The seventh speaks for itself all too cogently: "Death—that's your answer to everything. Jesus!"

When one moves to a new city, one's old address book no longer applies. One needs to find a new doctor, a new dentist, a new optician, a new accountant and a new lawyer. So far I have managed without the last two, but this net gain is cancelled out by my now needing rather more than one physician. On a more mundane level of annoyance, one realises that one no longer knows by heart the phone numbers of various taxi companies. Certainly one cannot tell in what district a telephone is located by looking at the prefix, as I could in Toronto, where I knew just what areas were comprised by, say, 362 and 364, exchanges I remember as being EMpire 2 and 3, long ago. In short, a person feels lonely, and this additional layer of melancholy, atop the thick compost of regret and hurt I was feeling as regards Cynthia, made me a disconsolate individual indeed. I was not blind to the significance that I read into the death notices and obituaries in the *Globe and Mail*.

Thinking more sunshine might do me good, I endeavoured to walk in both the morning and the late afternoon, using the time between for writing. I was usually outdoors to see the long drawn-out Vancouver sunset, when the sky to the west turned the same shade of orange as a Diamond taxi in Toronto (EMpire 6-6868) and seemed to be showing off, looking a little too perfect, as though the entire scene had been Photoshopped for some slick commercial purpose.

Everyone knows that Vancouver has no snow to speak of. What is less well understood is that in the summer conversely the city experiences no lightning and thunder. Something about the moderating effect of the ocean on one side and the mountains on the other preventing any collision of a warm air mass and a cold one. I found it uncomfortable and even eerie. Such things added to my disquiet. This in turn led to insomnia, which is how I came to write at night instead, only to discover that I actually had nothing to write about except Cynthia.

Sitting in what would be darkness were it not for the strange intergalactic glow of the monitor, I found I could concentrate. I began to write out every conversation she and I had had, at least every one that I could remember; and I found that I could recall most of them in minute detail, for the more I typed in the dialogue the more I had to add.

Parts of this material, some of it already in my head untranscribed, other parts newly recovered, were emblematic of the mess in which our couple-ness ended. What had she meant when she snapped that she didn't want "a co-dependent relationship"? Surely not what the term actually means—two people addicted to the same substance. Was she using it to mean that she feared she would have to take care of me during my slow physical decline? If so, that at least had the virtue of being brutally honest of course but brutally callow as well. Or was it intended to suggest some emotional weakness on my part? Either way, I don't see why she feared we would be headed towards *co*-dependence. What or whom was it that she herself was dependent upon? Nothing and no one as far as I could see, though she had her vulnerabilities like the rest of us. And then there was the final and definitive assertion that we have different values.

Was I educated/foreign/Jewish to her bootstraps/native-born/WASP? Or only one or two of these, or others entirely? In any event, why were such differences, whatever they might have been, a deal-breaker?

Faye and I had been married by a provincial court judge in the little Laura Ashley-inspired nondenominational (indeed, interfaith) chapel at Old City Hall, directly across the corridor from where people must go to check in with their parole officers. The two clienteles mingled in the crowded hallway as people waited their turns. Yet telling them apart was easy. Those about to be wed were often not obvious matches: Swedes were marrying Jamaicans, ethnic Chinese marrying southern Europeans, whites marrying Natives and so on. Surely such cultural differences made Cynthia's and mine seem insignificant. So we'll do a combined Christmas/Hanukkah, the two traditions shall be as one. My parents might be aghast, but other couples do it all the time, as I already had demonstrated once. I felt the values question was one I would puzzle over for the remainder of my life, such as it may be.

But the memory fragment to which I kept returning was when Cynthia told me about all the pornography one can find on the internet. I'm such an adept at this now and so jaded that I cannot recreate exactly the process of fumbling by which I entered this digital underground, hoping to relieve my solitude and desperation to be sure but also, I thought, to try understanding her by means of her largely secret desires. Was I deluding myself? Oh probably.

She had mentioned Google, so that is where I began. Cynthia was not one to blurt out her fantasies but I did have several clues and keywords. Typing them into the search engine produced screen after screen of crude and often nonsensical come-ons. I had blundered into the jungle of commercial websites. I realise what I am about to say will make me sound like an idiot, but I was new to the game I had resisted learning about for so long. Accordingly I thought "advanced search" would merely expand the scope and number of sites rather than narrow them. Figuring out what an advanced search does was my first discovery. Emboldened, I made the balletic leap to advanced searches in Groups and the door to the treasure vault swung open. In alt. and soc. were hundreds of sex groups, moderated and unmoderated, covering every imaginable practice, or any that I could have imagined back then. I thought: From what I know of her sexuality, and I guess I know it as well as anyone for she is either a very private person or (in a lustful way) a very reticent one, what key words or phrases would she most probably respond to? When on those precious few occasions she opened up, she did like to describe the art of fucking and of course her much-vaunted breasts. And she was unusually (I think) drawn to anal excitement, though she and I never tried anal sex (and I am sure that, because of my illness and its treatment, I lack the stamina for it today—I'd have to check). So I sought messages that combined *fucked* with *tits* and *anal,* learning soon to exclude messages with the word *gay,* and sat back and read the results, some of them "personals" but others disguised as true experiences. You cannot spend twenty-five years, as I had, reading people's manuscripts, first as an editor and then as an agent, without understanding the underlying motives revealed so blatantly in what was almost always such decidedly non-professional prose. Every night I would work at the computer until my eyes grew too weary to continue; sometimes my vision actually became blurred, as I somehow believed that I could learn more by moving closer to the impermanent words on the glass. I inspected them as I must have thought I would like to inspect her once again, stripping them naked, methodically, checking every square inch of them, probing them as deeply and slowly as I could whenever my fingers broke through into a hidden declivity of some sort, like a foot falling through a rotten step on a staircase in a haunted house. I wanted the prose bare-arsed and spread as wide as possible for my inspection. This was literary criticism with a purpose. Wet, not dry.

Of course it wasn't long before I discovered Yahoo "groups" and the "communities" at MSN and Lycos. Each had its advantages. Yahoo's had ease of access to all those pictures, though the company was forever shutting down groups for what seemed arbitrary reasons and gradually tightening up the rules, indeed restricting the whole process, like the bureaucracy that it was and is. Lycos had nice sites searchable by category and good resolution on the pictures but after a short time the engine, which is owned by a university in the American Midwest, decided to pull the plug and get out of the sex business entirely. MSN had the toughest entry restrictions and the smallest number of communities but allowed you to view the images in either scroll or grid fashion. I have long preferred the former.

I was aware that Cynthia was not particularly turned on by the graphic and the visual. Women generally are not, not to the same extent as men: a statement that owes its utility as a cliché to the fact that it is substantially true. While I personally enjoyed much of this pictorial confectionary, I knew that the amateurs were all too real to be exciting, while the models, male and female, were too well formed and too alike to be authentic. I was interested in combing methodically through the so-called discussion groups, the Google ones in particular, a gigantic undertaking, the genome of sex you might say, which was forever changing, being added to, and would not sit still for analysis; few things do in the virtual world. I would sift through all of it, researching sex stuff I remembered from our affair or was led to by instinct and intuition once I got a feel for the material and learned to trust my judgement in these matters. I would piece together Cynthia's sexual past, reconstruct her time with me and project it into the future. This may sound farfetched but this is what science does constantly, so why not homemade erotic literature? By reading the fantasies of the North American masses, I might gain some insights that would enable me to forego certain conjunctions, certain congruities. With what I knew about Cynthia, I would build the picture one pixel at a time. That is how it is done. I would call it sex profiling but the point is that it is not a profile at all, not some sort of crude schematic outline, but a picture that is rounded, multidimensional, fleshed out. I was like a painter mastering the manipulation of the picture plane, creating perspective and the illusion of depth.

For example, I remember Cynthia alluding, not apropos anything, to the fact that sperm is salty to the taste. "Like soup in a Greek restaurant", we joked. This one recollection alone gave me clues—keywords and clusters of keywords—from which to build another layer, to put on another coat of detail. You probably think this shows that I am obsessive, though I wasn't obsessing in the least, only enquiring, hoping eventually to understand her well enough to gain some understanding of what she thought of as co-dependency and of values that were not shared. Maybe I would find that mere methodologies and not systems of belief were what we failed to have in common. When I confront a problem, an event, an episode, an untoward occurrence, my instinct is to impose a grid on the site, then look at the situation contextually, referentially, comparing it to other such happenings or messes in the past, hoping to puzzle the thing out. In contrast, her first reaction was to fly into a temper, calling people names that I hope in my case she really did not mean. What more could I do in the absence of the person herself than to engage in the sort of forensics I am describing? What more could I do given her refusal to communicate in any way?—though once I thought there might be a break in the ice or at least the possibility of one, a setting in which a conversation might be nurtured.

I didn't have much to do with the publishing world any more beyond a little editing, a bit of teaching and even less consulting. But for some reason I was given two tickets to a cocktail reception at the Vancouver Public Library, that ruined Roman amphitheatre of a building memorialising the ruination of European culture. The occasion was the induction of new people into the literary walk of fame, a series of plaques on the pavement outside on which unheeding passers-by scuff their feet. Having no one to go with, I left the other invitation at home. When I arrived and checked my coat, I went to the admissions table to pick up my name tag. There in the next row of the alphabet I saw one with her name. It jumped out at me as though it were in red ink and italic while all the others were black and roman. All through the ceremony I kept turning round to see if she was among the latecomers, but she did not materialise. Had another engagement come up after she had répondez-vous'd in the affirmative? Or had she heard that I was going to be there and cancelled out? Perhaps she had merely intuited my presence. I felt I had to hurry home and consult my database, the I Ching of Cynthia I seemed to be writing for my own semi-mystical purposes.

※ ※ ※

I have never accommodated myself to pronouncing Strachan as Stracken the way people do out here rather than Strawn. I have never quite grown accustomed to putting the apartment or office number in front of the street number rather than behind it when addressing envelopes. When I was young I knew that I finally had left England behind for Canada when I decided North Americans were correct to distinguish *which* from *that*. Although I continue to struggle, I have found it more difficult to embrace the idea that marks of punctuation should be inside and not outside quotation marks when they are not actually part of that which is being quoted. But I am an adaptable person all the same and have found that I enjoy the copyediting style of the *Economist* in the matter of using double quotation marks around single ones, not vice versa, though in what you are reading I will no doubt be at the mercy of someone else's slowly evolved house style. All that said, I am not completely of the West and even now am still not able to accept turning to any other paper than the *Globe and Mail* for death notices and obituaries. For one thing, I don't know enough Vancouver people to comprehend the obit page of the *Vancouver Sun*. Occasionally I recognise a surname, but these are not people I know as individuals, whereas people who die in the *Globe* have passed a test of familiarity with one sector of the public or another and all too often, with growing regularity in fact, are individuals I myself have known or met or did business with for years. When someone's passing is acknowledged in the *Globe*, then the person is dead officially. They have survived the test of living and gone to their microfilmed reward. My thoughts on this matter came to a head early the following January when Father phoned to say that Mother had had a stroke. He seemed to be fearing the worst and so naturally I followed his example.

He was audibly upset of course but strangely he didn't seem to me any sadder than he did ordinarily. Perhaps sadness had not had time to triumph over shock. Perhaps his style of going about living in the world had always been infused with sadness. The call came in the morning before I was even fully caffeinated. Even though the weather in Toronto was especially fierce at the time and many flights were being cancelled or delayed, I managed to board an afternoon one that adhered to the schedule remarkably well. As I sat there wedged into the seat, I could imagine the funeral that must be coming. I presumed the two of them must have discussed ritual matters at some point in their shared old age. I supposed that I ought to get Father to make known to me his own wishes for when his turn comes, but of course I would hesitate to ask any time soon when he might be headed into mourning his—our—loss. Later, possibly about the moment we were over Winnipeg, it occurred to me that in light of my cancer he was undoubtedly having the same thoughts about me, his only son, childless and now wifeless as well. In talking around such topics over the next two weeks we did, however, manage to cover some of the other important issues.

"You mother invested in me," he said. This struck me as an odd way of saying what he meant, especially for him, someone with no skill at business because he had no interest in it, condemning himself to a succession of faltering small enterprises to keep the household functioning the whole time I was growing up. When we first arrived in Canada, he sold Scots goods—kilts and sporrans and such, not to mention bagpipes. The fact is typically absurd, given that he of course had no more connection to that culture than a daughter-in-law of Caledonian extraction way in the future and that the market for such things was drying up in a Toronto where one no longer had to be a member of the Orange Lodge to get a part-time job at the public library on College Street and police recruiters no longer went to the Gorbals in Glasgow each year to entice entire street gangs into becoming Metro constables.

"Most women just pick someone who seems the most acceptable and try their best to keep the relationship in good repair," he said. "Eventually she finds the husband wanting. She hates herself for ruining her chances and ends up hating him too. It's like the eternal question of the money-men: When to sell when you can't foresee the market? All you can see are some temporary trends, if you're lucky." Why was he using all this financial language? I didn't know. "But she went in for the whole thing. She's in it right to the end."

His voice was flat with fatigue, perhaps from too much emotion, but otherwise it was the same voice I had been talking with by phone all those months, the same one I remember being reared by. But looking at him now I suddenly saw that his mouth had grown old. It had begun to shrink around the edges, like a pool of water evaporating before my eyes. I wondered how he was going to do on his own if she did not pull through. I could learn the answer only as time went on of course.

I think my own reaction to Mother's stroke differed from what it would have been before my surgery—more extreme, yet I was less upset as well. This may sound odd, but it's true. I have danced with death. Having been introduced to it, however, I had a relationship with it that could not be understood by those who had not yet made its acquaintance. I had not died, but I was part of the dead-elect, a concept most if not all healthy people are unable to comprehend (but they will, in time).

Toronto was having some of its worst winter weather in memory, at least in the memory of people no longer young but not yet completely old. The snow was deep, and the top powdery layer was constantly being blown through the architectural canyons. Visibility was extraordinarily low and in any case further limited by the hood of the parka I was finally forced to buy if I were going to get round. Toronto had had a terrible summer. It was the summer of SARS and other public health concerns that had eroded the city's economy. Now it was having a terrible winter, with the sort of temperatures that give one a headache after a few minutes' exposure and make frostbite a real danger and actually cause some of the homeless to suffer hypothermia and then freeze. Certainly I remembered nothing like it when I was a young fellow, not sustained like this, but then my recollection was being assaulted by the thought that it could not any longer be trusted.

I had been gone only two years but in that time the city had become more like Bangkok than I could possibly have imagined. There was madness everywhere. How could this have happened? The city's metabolism had run amok. Many of the landmarks I once knew had disappeared as completely as a ship at sea that sinks below the waves with nothing to mark where it had been. I began to feel what I imagined my parents must have experienced crossing borders, except that mine were borders of time. Time was a runaway locomotive, destroying everything in its path. I was of course staying in the old apartment where I once had been a teenager, and the *ping-ping* of the ice pellets striking the windowpanes seemed to call attention less to conditions outside than to the sorrow and apprehension within. I got zipped into my parka and put on Father's rubber snow boots and took the subway downtown.

Inside the train the concept of time was distorted even more wildly.

Office workers, dripping wet, were abandoning desks and going home an hour early, so many of them that it was a rush hour of those attempting to avoid the rush hour. Yet the corners of the car were filled with those who seemed more like late-night passengers: derelicts with the fare in their pocket, asleep with their heads in their laps as though in a posture suitable for yoga or vomiting, and kids with plenty of jewellery, none of it on their fingers or round their necks, wearing also the expression of arrogant goofiness that the drugs seemed to dress them in. People got off to transfer to the Bloor line and later to board GO trains at Union Station at the bottom of the loop. The light had a quality I had never seen on the trains before, the eerie green of bottle glass, the blue of sparks in an electrical fire, the red of a warning button suddenly brought alive by some unknown disaster. I felt ill, vaguely yet unequivocally, and got off at Spadina, the gateway to all life forms, and trudged outside where visibility was intermittent at best. I was cold and my nose was running and my eyes tearing from the cold, but I was all right; I had all the breath I required.

I made my way westward along Bloor. Some things were just as they had been when I had seen them last. The church built in the age of faith had been taken over by various homespun crisis centres, support groups, and hotlines: a shopping mall of the spirit, full of draughty rooms with vaulted ceilings. The former bank branches, designed in the era when banks peddled the idea of security rather than the illusion of convenience, were now, in the epoch of the ATM and online usury, functioning as restaurants and pubs. Other things were distressingly absent altogether. The old drugstore was gone. It had been run for nearly fifty years by a thin hollow-cheeked man who had acted as the de facto doctor or at least medical advisor for generations of European immigrants. I can remember seeing elderly women, exiled with headscarves, who shunned Shoppers Drug Mart up the street because it was so new and too confusing and everyone spoke English too quickly, whereas Abe, as he was known to all, ran a small cramped shop full of strange patent medicines and abdominal trusses, cheap cosmetics and yellowing dog-eared greeting cards suitable for a great many but not all occasions, and could if necessary listen to testimony about your aches and pains in Yiddish or Hungarian as well as English. I think he must have died at just about the same time as the last of his long-time customers. I wished his spirit peace and felt inexpressibly alone in the world.

I turned up Bathurst, one of those streets up which people like my parents, and other Europeans before them and West Indians afterwards, ascended as they found their assigned roles in the native-born anglos' aspirations. Tacky, physically dirty old Bathurst, always trying to come up in the world and always failing, was like an archaeological site illustrating occupation by successive cultures. The Vietnamese bridal shop with its teeny tiny gowns, the market where you could buy goat meat and copies of the *Gleaner* direct from Jamaica, the strange Turkish coffee house or club where men with what looked like Saddam Hussein moustaches played a gambling game like dominoes using white ceramic tiles that looked as though they might have come from some ancient gents' lavatory, the fake South Asian vegetarian restaurant where shaved-headed young Protestant kids in saris and robes left you alone before taking your order in the hope you might be forced to read some of their guru's inspirational (to them at least) literature. But between and among all these familiar spots were deep black wells of change.

The wind was rushing down from the north but I fought my way up to Dupont. The snow was turning to sleet and coming down in an oblique curtain, so thickly that it almost obscured the interrogation lighting inside the diner that boasted on its sign of having been REPUTABLE SINCE 1955. One always suspected that in fact the place had been in business since the Depression but for the first generation had been somewhat dodgy. Faye and Gunnar evidently lived somewhere to the west where the houses were smaller and the accents thicker but where each year renovators like themselves were reclaiming more and more of the territory as their own. Instead, I turned east and broke a trail towards the old neighbourhood Faye and I had shared. Getting there took an inordinately long time as the snow was now heavier as well as deeper, and with each step I pulled up great clods of it on Father's old boots. I rounded the right corner, however, and saw from an entirely new angle the strange little house we had known as home. I withdrew more deeply into the tunnel-like hood of the parka lest one of the old neighbours recognise me and the embarrassing secret of my sentimental mission become known. But there was no one else abroad that evening, understand-ably enough. I ventured closer like an anxious animal not quite trusting its prey to stay dead. At the foot of the flagstone walk, now entombed under deep snow, I stopped a moment to look up at the upper storey where the windows were rectangles of dirty yellow light. I was aware that this was the first time I was looking at the place as a stranger. Its body was the same but its soul had changed hands. Perhaps women leave houses without admitting regret, the way they leave marriages, vowing never to speak a civil word to the building ever again for as long as they both shall live. But I cannot and do not wish to. Just then the front door opened and a chap I had never seen before, youngish, tall, wearing a bulky Irish pullover, stepped halfway outside and deposited empty wine bottles in the blue recycling bin. He saw me standing there and gave me a proprietary glance. But what could he have seen at that distance on such a night? Only a nonexistent face far back in the hood of the parka that was a bit to large for him, with rubber wellies a bit too small, a middle-aged Jew from a long line of same who have never moved anywhere but just keep escaping from place to place, one step ahead of themselves.

✳ ✳ ✳

"I was sorry to hear about your mother's illness."

"How did you hear?"

"I ran into Eleanor Sims."

Pam and I were in a coffee shop round the corner from the office she had rented on Spadina Avenue, which had become the High Street of independent publishing. In my parents' time, the prewar office buildings were full of cutters, fitters, furriers, people selling ladies' ready-to-wear. The very name Spadina meant the shmatte business as surely as Bay Street meant the stock exchange. Now the Jews had been displaced by prosperity, assimilation, low tariffs on imports, and centrifugal force. Forever either a ghetto or a diaspora.

"I wonder where she got the news?"

Pam shrugged her broad shoulders a bit, as if to say "Beats me." As though to warm herself, for indeed it was still cold though the snow of the past few days had abated and the stuff in the streets, what hadn't been cleared away, was already turning black, she put her hands round her mug of coffee (she had brought her own from the office, I guess to keep from asking for refills). She looked just as blonde, big-boned, healthy and well adjusted as always but of course was wearing clothes I had never seen her in before. What else had she changed into in her life? For a moment, I felt like Jason returning with the Argonauts or Crusoe finally leaving the island for a home now terrifying in its strangeness.

I purposely didn't want to see the new premises lest I make myself sad and make her feel I was checking up on her. These were essentially the same reasons I never asked about the dog, not wanting to hear that he had died. Yet I was entitled to ask about the health of the business, in which I was still after all a silent investor.

"Well, no clients have dropped away," she said with a little laugh I suddenly remembered was one of her signatures. "Not all of them are productive, though. I tried to find a couple of other good ones. The royalties still click by on time, but the problem seems to be getting advances spread out evenly through the year to meet monthly expenses."

I shook my head. "That's always been the difficulty, for all agents everywhere."

"So I've gone from building websites for people to also being webmaster for a few small presses. They're not clients of the agency and never will be, so I don't see any conflict."

"Neither do I."

"And I hope I can get the contract for one of the associations as well. I mean, I'm right here in the middle of the publishing ghetto." I thought how my father would have reacted to the word, but of course I didn't so much as let one hair betray me. "And I know the industry. So I guess you could say I'm subsidising myself until the agency grows."

"Sounds good to me. It's a plan." She betrayed just the slightest sign of relief. She also seemed surprised when I said websites was the other reason I was eager to see her. She of course knew me only as a technophobe or at the very least someone with no talent in the area whatever or even basic know-how (a fact I always half-suspected she thought had been holding the agency back).

"Would you be willing to sell a bit of your knowledge?"

She smiled and looked at her mug. "Knowledge comes cheap. You can buy it with a coffee."

I told her I was interested in having my own website.

"That's easy."

"No, I'd like to know how I can get someone to teach me to run it myself."

"Hmm." I could not accurately decipher this but assumed she was quietly amused, as though an especially clumsy friend who had never studied medicine had asked her to teach him surgery.

"You see, I want to create all the material myself and then moderate discussions."

"Is this for the fiction you're hoping to write? I was going to ask you how you were coming with that of course."

I guess I hesitated a micro-second before answering. "Sort of."

"You said 'moderated'. Would this be a commercial site?"

"No, I thought it would be like something on Yahoo groups. For discussion. With people applying to join but not paying for the service."

She was sweet not to make sport of me. "Ah, well that's not a website in the strict sense but a group as you say, a kind of online club really. In fact, they used to be called clubs—Excite Clubs, for instance. I wouldn't think you'd have to study very hard to do that. Would it carry advertising, though, to bring in a little money?"

"I suppose it could, when it got big enough, if it ever did—if there were anybody who wanted to advertise."

She was of course far ahead of me. Her lips were steady but I thought her eyes were preparing for an inwardly focused smile. "Do you see much visual content?"

"Oh yes."

"Would it be a substantial part of it?"

I said yes, probably.

"And you'd archive messages and they'd be searchable?"

"That's how I saw it."

"None of this sounds too difficult. Or unusual. Let me go to Yahoo and figure out what arrangements they offer, what's acceptable to them. Then if you like I can email you all the information, telling you how to get started. Then you're on your own. Of course you can always call me if you ever have problems. But these things are very common. Very popular."

I thanked her and willed my face not to turn red, and she steered the conversation back to where it had begun. "How's your father bearing up?"

"Quite well. He was shocked of course. Not amazed. There had been signs, but one's always surprised by the timing when it does happen. He always thought he'd be the one to get sick first, but Mother, as I say, had been having some difficulties for a while, but we thought medication was controlling the problem. When I got the call telling me about the stroke, I jumped on the plane. Believe me, I thought I was coming back for a service at Beth Sinai."

"And what's the prognosis?"

"Didn't Eleanor tell you?" I said this just to be mischievous; I couldn't help myself, but my words were free of even a homeopathic trace of anything accusatory. "The doctors say she's recovered more, and more quickly, than anyone would have suspected. She still hobbles quite severely but her speech is fairly good. Much of it sounds a bit odd because her mouth is drawn to one side. How quickly one recovers from this point shows how much permanent damage there is, but as the doctors keep saying, nobody can know much for certain until it happens. She's getting great treatment, I think. Father wants to take care of her himself, and he's doing a fine job so far, from what I see. Sounds odd, but it's given him something important to do every day, which he hasn't had in a while. I think the lack of something like that was beginning to weaken him as well. Now he's perkier than ever." Pam smiled at *perkier*. "He has someone he can fuss over endlessly who really needs the fussing, which frankly I suspect is as important as physio."

"Sounds like it could have been a lot worse."

"Other people's relationships are always incomprehensible from the outside, you know how it is. Even with one's own parents one never really has a clue. *Especially* with one's own parents. But I think they've had an endlessly adaptable sort of marriage. This is just the latest version. Maybe the final one of course but right now it's just the latest."

As I was saying this, I was trying to decide whether she had seen or heard anything of Faye or Faye-and-Gunnar. I couldn't seem to come up with a line of enquiry that was neither too obvious nor too subtle. So I asked lamely whether she had seen any of my old Toronto friends. What she answered surprised me to an extent I do not think I was terribly successful at disguising.

"Deirdre Estep always asks about you. She has Blair's unfinished novel of course. I've read it and, you know, it's not all that unfinished, not at all. Of course he would have taken it further, but it's not short and it's quite fully realised as it is. He was obviously one of those writers who rewrote every page however many times he had to, before moving on to the next one. Deirdre has a lot of other unpublished stuff as well and some of it's quite interesting. And of course she's got the rights back to the others. So she and I meet every now and then to talk about the literary estate, toss ideas around, make plans. She's a pretty smart woman. Turns out she has a real knack for being a literary executrix. I think there'll be some news on this soon."

I thought carefully about what to say. "I'm surprised she remembers me. I was much closer to Blair. Faye and I would see them socially from time to time, but for the most part any business relationship the agency had with Blair was an extension of our friendship, the two us." That sounded a trifle lame. "We would go the gym together, sometimes twice a week." Ever lamer.

"Anyway, she speaks very warmly of you."

※ ※ ※

When strangers, hearing the faintest suggestion of an inauthentic vowel, ask me where I am "from" or where I "grew up", my initial response, which is never said out loud of course, is: "You're absolutely correct, you were born here and I was not and I can never be your equal as a human being, I couldn't agree more." In the end, everything either rises to the level of language or sinks to the level of language.

People who have always spoken English as easily as Oscar Peterson plays the piano cannot credit the struggles that a person from outside must undergo. I cannot forget the memory of washing up in England without English. The syntax and grammar, eccentric as they are, came to me easily enough in time, largely through conversation of course but also through conscious study. I am of the generation that was taught how to parse a sentence. Strangely, the subtleties of vocabulary, shall we call them, were more difficult. Homonyms were sometimes problematic, not to mention words that were merely somewhat alike. I remember being corrected, more openly than I felt necessary, for confusing *boost* and *boast*, with the result that years afterwards I avoid both words as well as the acts they represent. Other embarrassments were *furtive* and *fertile, hideout* and *hide-away, backtrack* and *back-pedal*. In fact, words and expressions using prepositions, or using them as adverbs, were a minefield. I could *put up* with something I was not *put out* by, as when a shopkeeper is forced to *close up* and have a *close-out* sale once his creditors *close in*. A *come-on*, you say? Ah, *come off* it. My puzzlement continued on another even more idiomatic plane when we came to Toronto. *How it's coming* [along]? versus *How's it going*, eh? All such usages could be perfected only in the tournament of daily communications. As I might express it in the world I inhabit now, "Why should a man be sheepish about feeling a bit goatish so long as he doesn't make a horse's ass of himself?"

Having put so much of my vital energy into the English language, to the point of becoming the friend, advisor, editor and eventually the agent of so many fine Canadian writers, I faced the cyberworld with terror at what I might find there and occasionally horror at what in fact I did stumble upon.

For the first few months I spent three, four, five or even six hours a night searching the porn sites. I knew at once what Cynthia would never have been interested in for a second. So I quickly eschewed anything bearing on bukakke, chloroform, bald-headed women, smoking or Japanese rope bondage. But the same instinct told me that were she here with me she would find that scenes as various as, for example, glory-holes, nurses and vintage catfights might pique interests she had not realised she had. I certainly suspected strongly, given certain aspects of her personality, that OTK (F/m but even F/f), milking, CFNM and femdom generally defined would speak to her fundamentally. So, I thought, would the various flat-chested sites. And of course I actually knew about her ebony longings, so the scores of interracial sites were a boon to my investigation and analysis. All of these keywords could be joined together in almost infinite combinations. For example, there were repositories of exquisite solitary pleasure about small-breasted women wearing glasses being nailed by black women with dildos or, conversely, white Protestant women like herself being taken sequentially or en masse by muscular black males while their white male partners—Jewish? who could rule out the possibility?—were strapped in chairs from which they watched the action.

My memory seemed to expand and ripen as the need for it grew. After even Vancouver had gone to bed, I would sometimes, through a process not unlike self-hypnosis, arrive at the stage where I could retrieve, with what seemed to me total aural accuracy, every word that she and I had spoken to each other over the course of a year, every casual uninflected utterance and every ululating and unguarded line of our phone-sex sessions. So equipped I would begin my two-pronged attack. First, I found the relevant Yahoo groups to join and sometimes MSN ones as well, picking out the fantasies of other solitary people in other darkened cities that matched the shape of the puzzle-pieces still missing. Then by using the links on each I found related sites, until my total climbed steadily to two hundred, four hundred, six hundred and finally nearly eight hundred groups, so many that a good deal of time was required, once in the morning and again at night, to scroll through the three or four thousand messages a day posted to them. Most of these groups were of course overwhelmingly photographic in nature, many including video archives. In a few of them, however, the photo inventory never seemed to change, especially after that fateful August thirteenth, a date incised in the memory of researchers such as myself along with all the lurkers and lechers of the world, when Yahoo simply forbade members from posting attachments to the groups, so that the only new images one would see were uploaded by the moderators or emailed by members. But a few groups were textually oriented. Tellingly, these included some of the most popular ones, with memberships well into the five figures. I am not taking into account all the foreign-language groups to which I eventually belonged, many in languages such as Italian and German with which I had only a glancing acquaintance. By going to them every day, however, I did begin to pick up the Italian slang relating to exhibitionism and the German nomenclature of, of course, BD and D/s—to say nothing of such ritualistic specialties as Verhöre and Leibesvisitationen, which fall under the broad heading WIP.

My other source of jigsaw bits was the text-only world of the Google newsgroups that Cynthia herself had told me of. Beginning with the ones she had brought up, then moving on to synonyms and rephrasings, I searched dozens of words and word strings at one sitting, turning up matches a hundred at a time in the labyrinthine corridors of alt. and soc. The stories were pure fantasy, virtually all of them, though occasionally one came across a supposedly real-life account that might, just might, have been just that. What most characterised this enormous floating continent of words was the poor quality of the writing. I remember being perplexed by US English when I first came to North America, refusing like so many English people to believe that it is in fact a separate tongue until the evidence was laid before me every day and in all media. Signs should be erected at the border: "Abandon adverbs all ye who enter here. Please drive safe." Of course I read American books, but these internet effusions are the real language of America, written without artifice, whether upward or downward, by people incapable of anything else. This is the crabbed ungrammatical language of the little dots of light one sees from the window seat at thirty thousand feet when one is flying between one brightly glowing conurbation and another. There were certainly groups that valued decent amateur prose, simple but clear, like that of the more careful newspapers. In some groups, individual writers, of course using pseudonyms or nicknames or the equivalent of graffiti artists' tags (for no one on the net, myself included, uses his or her true name) evidently acquired loyal followings, rather like professional athletes. Other members might write in response about the qualities of a writer's story they particularly admired or failed to admire. In a way, this was following the enviable principle of adult education, built with porn instead of the Everyman's Library. One could not imagine a middle-class English version of this editorial process: "I say, nice job on the soccer mum with tanlines and her face covered in man jam. Made my pecker take the salute, it did."

But the level of knowledge, this was the thing I found disturbing. The people had trouble expressing themselves even in the simplest terms in their vocabularies of perhaps a couple of thousand words. Their thoughts were of course crude. This was after all pornography.

But the -graphy fell way short of the porno-. These men could do no more than transcribe what they were speaking under their breath. I could visualise them setting the words down as their lips moved in unison with the progress of the rough block letters or the childlike cursive, often without end punctuation or paragraphing, just as it would have been uttered aloud. The most remarkable thing to me was that they cared not enough about how they presented themselves through language even to put what they had written through a cursory spell-check before posting it where it might remain forever in inherently impermanent form.

In this trackless sexual underground that in fact is not underground at all but simmers above us like a sky of sexual emptiness, the two most commonly misspelled words are *cloths* for clothes and, often in the same sentence, *striped* for stripped. The plural *wifes* follows in third place, I would say. Reading these again and again every night, I concluded that we may have been mistaken to suppose that people in the distant past, before orthography came to be standardised and certainly before recorded sound, pronounced words in the same now-quaint ways they spelled them. Now I doubt that Chaucer sounded Chaucerian at all. The anonymous authors whose work I met with every night surely did not say *wifes* for wives. They wrote as they did because—well, why exactly? Because they had disdain for rudimentary education or more likely had been denied it or lived almost entirely through televised pictures or simply did not care. Yet they felt their terrible animating desire to communicate what they found most interesting to think about: sex. I concluded that they must use sex—the fantasies of sex on demand and in all its multifarious forms—the same way others, wretched in different ways perhaps, used alcohol, drugs and violence: to protest against the numbing pain of living.

I wasn't fool enough to believe I could raise standards, not even in my little corner of the outlaw galaxy. But I could create a site that would attempt to set a higher example of imagination and of writing, hoping in that way, through the exploration of genuine literary erotica, to attract women to participate as well as men. Certified women, not men utterly and comically unable to disguise their gender much less their sensibilities: an all-too-common type on web communities. As though they could possibly fool someone who has read thousands of novels as I have. As though they deceive anybody in fact.

All those years in publishing had convinced me that I was on the wrong side of the desk, that I had greater skill as a writer than the people whose manuscripts I edited or peddled. Divorce, disease and abandonment seemed to be compelling me to take my life westward and use whatever time might remain to me for writing some—however much I could—of the fiction I should have been producing all along. After a couple of years, however, the pain was still too great for me to make any real progress. (Blame the pain and not the wound. Such is our way.) In truth, either I simply did not have the talent or I was incapable of making art from my injuries by trying to heal them, as I have known so many writers to do. Instead I would write of erotic longing (not obsession, please) and in doing so hope to find answers to the questions: Why did she dump me? How did I fail her? And having shed herself of me, why could she not consent to a cordial imitation friendship based on the intensity of our shared past and simple good manners? Why was she so angry all the time, before, during and apparently afterwards? I felt that the key was understanding more of her sexuality than I had done when we were a couple. To go deeply into her mind from a distance of time and space and emerge with the beginnings of a plausible answer to any of these conundrums, that was the plan. By doing so, I could hasten the regenerative process by making the most accomplished erotic prose I could after first creating my own environment for it. I had an audience. There must be more people like me who enjoy careful writing. I had the skill. Look at all the guttural often post-literate stuff from which I could so easily distinguish what I did.

One night I had a dream that first promised to be upsetting but soon turned marvellous, a sort of madcap sixties movie of a dream, giving in to the youthful craziness to which its own narrative momentum and improvised structure led it, rather like *What's New, Pussycat?* or *Casino Royale*. Father enlists Blair Estep, Pam and me and someone else—someone from Vancouver, I cannot tell who—in a search for lost treasure. But we are being followed. Along the way, Father and Blair become misplaced, leaving me and the other two to have many zany escapades, including narrow misses in squalid hotels and quick getaways in an enormous white caravan with Pam at the wheel. In the end, we locate the treasure trove in the brick cellar of some old industrial building in the North of England full of service tunnels with hidden entrances. The treasure turns out to be first Father and then Blair, both safe and sound. Reunited, we make a combined run for it, our finale.

This would have made a wonderful dream for recounting to Shrink A or Shrink B back in Toronto or to both of them in fact, to use as a control surface or baseline to weigh their differing reactions and their varying levels of professional redundancy. It woke me up and I made note of the time—six thirty-two. I threw my feet over the edge of the bed and experienced a revelation of sorts. Suddenly it struck me with great clarity just what makes pornography so pornographic. Not sex surely but the fact that porn characters undergo such violent or degrading experiences yet are completely unfazed by them. At the end of the story they are precisely the same people they were at the beginning despite all they have been through in the middle. They are cripples because they cannot communicate, as one must do in order to change, grow or even survive. We are all characters in a dirty story written by God or someone.

※ ※ ※

When I was getting into business in Toronto in the early eighties, the city was full of melancholic Montreal anglophones fleeing separatism, the language laws, the scorn of the majority. They made a sad presence in Ontario, wandering disconsolately from party to party and lunch to lunch, self-indulgent victims of their own exile sentimentality. Some were Jews who had added anti-Semitism, or at least the fear of it, to the outrages they were escaping. But all of them reminded me of Jews of my parents' generation, their feet in one place but their hearts in another one their memories could not shake. But by the time I am remembering now, Toronto was the new Montreal and people were leaving it before it actually collapsed on top of them or because they felt they were owed a better climate as a reward for lifetime achievement. I met these ex-Torontonians everywhere I went in my microenvironment, and I saw myself in their reflection. Stalin infamously called the Jews "rootless cosmopolitans". The phrase was hardly a compliment of course but it kept recurring to me as the neatest way to describe the new arrivals in neutral language. To my astonishment, one of these people was a major figure from my past. Here is what happened.

It was the last week of July, the time of what is now called, in trite grandiose fashion, the Celebration of Light. This is one of five holidays on the calendar of the West End, which starts with the Polar Bear Swim every January first. The swim has gone on since the 1920s at English Bay Beach where scores or perhaps a hundred otherwise responsible people put on bathing suits and run into the frigid surf, submerging themselves and their self-doubts for a moment, then rush back out to change before foolhardiness degenerates to the level of actual physical danger. A thick crowd of people comes to cheer and hoot while getting a glimpse of live uncovered flesh, a commodity in as short supply during the rainy winter months as it is too overabundant in the summer ones. The Swim tides everyone over until June when crowds reassemble for the Dragon Boat Races. This is a more recent tradition but one the citizens—the ones who go to the symphony at the Orpheum but applaud between movements—have taken to with childlike alacrity, because it is closer to a sporting event than a cultural one. Then the Celebration of Light fireworks extravaganza follows in midsummer.

To a greater or lesser extent than the other two major religious observances—Pride Day around August first and Halloween at the end of October—the fireworks draw shoulder-to-shoulder crowds of drunks, brawlers and pickpockets, not simply the people of the neighbourhood. That may be partly because unlike the equivalent displays of waste in Montreal and Toronto, Vancouver's fireworks are free. On each of the four nights—two Wednesdays and two Saturdays—the awe-struck begin arriving at dinner time to stake out their viewing positions. When the sky is sufficiently dark, the pyrotechnicians start igniting the displays loaded on a barge in the middle of English Bay. The explosions are timed to emphasise the symphonic twists and turns of the music being played. The Celebration is actually more of a competition, for each night's spectacle is themed to a different country. The noise and the music are thunderous and almost interminable. My first summer in Vancouver, I remember, I lay on the bed with all the windows closed and listened to the sky popping and erupting in what to my depressive ears sounded like a cross between a rock concert and an air raid.

Of course I'm describing this now as a hardened sybaritic Vancouverite, but at the time I was actually eager for the impending excitement, which I thought should set me up perfectly for a night-long session with the porno muse. I tried to arrive early enough to secure a good vantage point across from the Sylvia, but the crowds were assembling from all directions, moving as though on invisible wheels instead of feet. Some people carried drinks coolers. Many were in outfits they trusted were outrageous. One young woman was so very nearly topless as to render the distinction meaningless; her hair was the same shade of blue as a MacLure's taxi ("Vancouver's finest"). Vendors of soft drinks and spicy sausages were doing a gold-rush business. People were howling in imitation of animals they had seen only in captivity. I could see across the water that an equivalent mob was taking shape in Vanier Park. Kitsilano still always made me remember Cynthia's basement suite. Suddenly the night was much darker than it had been only two minutes earlier. Soon there would be the first blast of music from the loudspeakers and the first little flash in the sky as though some amorphous all-knowing deity were taking a quick Polaroid. At exactly that moment someone astern of my left ear loudly called my name. I turned and saw Eleanor Sims. She looked like a woman who had put a great deal of thought into what to wear to an orgy of fireworks.

"Eleanor, what are you doing here?" I had to shout for now the sky was a giant video screen of cluster bombs trailing red, yellow and green streamers as they ascended, flourished all too briefly, then disintegrated in little apologetic puffs.

"I live here now!" Her voice carried better than mine over the tumult. "I came out a few months ago and bought a place. Not far. I've been hoping I might see you. Hearing a lot about you."

"And I've been hearing about me *from* you." But my voice was too deep for the words to compete with all the blossoms of thunder. No doubt that was just as well. In any case, the conversation was becoming more telegraphic by the second. This was hardly the setting for a discussion.

"Give me your number." I had to half-scream this and she had to half-lip-read. She plunged one hand into her bag and returned with a pen and a scrap of paper. She had to write in big slow numbers in the dark, as though she were tracing them.

"Call me. All right? I mean it!" She was smiling as the crowd ate her up.

*** *** ***

Even after all the time that had elapsed since the move, I was still sometimes disoriented, not knowing which place I was in. Disoriented in small ways. Someone's name would flit across the surface of my brain and I would have to take a second to remember in which place they lived. Once when, I admit, I was pretty groggy, having been up most of the night in the human cyberzoo where midnight is perpetual, I overheard someone in the next booth say sharply, "Just because they call it all-day breakfast don't mean you get all day to eat it"—and I knew instantly that I was in Vancouver, not the other place. The trip back to Toronto the previous winter had been strange enough to jar loose some of the crust that seemed to prevent swift movement of my neurons. After all I had expected to return from there in a state of mourning, which is one of the strongest and most firmly affixed emotions and perhaps one of the most necessary. Whatever happened back there had happened partly by not happening (there I go again, starting to sound like a follower of the Kitsilano school of Buddhist thought). What happened there caused me to think even more about the pre-Cynthian past. By the same token it made me see my new surroundings differently as their newness wore off. At first Vancouver seemed to me as all of Canada once did, full of strangeness worth taming through knowledge. Did the people here really grow up knowing all this stuff I was now coming to know but differently because of my late arrival? I envied but could not quite believe those who had always been assimilated into this landscape of summer and the Somerset Maugham rain of winter, who had never actually experienced any but passive-aggressive weather. I felt the need to talk with someone, an actual human, not a fake identity sitting at a keyboard like mine at some undisclosed location in some country they weren't always prepared to identify. So, in the absence of anyone I could trust, I gave Eleanor a ring.

She was still at the happy stage of being settled in a new place and compiling, through an exacting process of trial and error, a little directory of restaurants she would consider going back to again. A place on the south side of Robson was evidently on the probationary list, pending final accreditation. The dinner date turned out to be the third most important meeting of my life, after the first time I ever saw Faye (or Fay, as she then was, before an unsuccessful rebellion against Protestantism led her to add the heretical final letter) and of course my initial conversation with Cynthia. In fact it may even be number two.

The restaurant was one of those places with a perfectly decent chef (they grow here in the warm soil) but poorly trained staff, the sort who interrupt conversation in the middle of the punch-lines and whisk away one person's plate before the other has stopped eating. Eleanor was in black and yellow, with a brooch of beaten silver, possibly Native, possible a symbolic sunburst. As always she looked as though she had stepped out of the window display of a rather smart shop. Perhaps knowing of my comparatively straitened circumstances, she had insisted on the phone that this would be her shout, as the Aussies say. Accordingly she suggested a particular Chilean wine unknown to me and ordered a bottle for us. Memory being what it is, this naturally gave me pause. But I need not have worried. This time her bombshell came not from the grape.

For a while we chatted about why she had changed cities. She said she was finding it difficult to write in Toronto any longer. "Far too many writers there already. No one can concentrate for all the talk about writing all the time." This sounded of course like an answer intended to deflect the question. More likely a sentimental attachment, I thought, but then I really know nothing whatever about her romantic life. Probably no one does except whoever is involved in it with her. Then we moved on to the scene back east, with which I was almost completely out of touch by this time.

"You've heard the news about Bob Mulligan?"

I had not. In fact, I had not heard his name or barely thought of him since giving up first the agency and then my own shall we say more traditional literary ambitions.

"After your friend Blair killed himself, the person who'd canned him got fired too. Makes you think Blair overreacted, doesn't it?" I'm not certain if I blanched at the supreme flippancy of that, but I certainly winced internally. "So the new executive producer revamped the format—and named Mulligan as host. You really mean you didn't read about all this in the *Globe*?"

"I mostly just look at the obituaries." I imagined how the last part of that sounded. I'm not certain I conveyed what I meant to say. I let it pass. It was hardly worth a long psychological explanation.

"He's in his element," she said. "He doesn't have to write any more. He just has to look as though he's about to, in some falling-down fit of inspiration, like one of the Romantic poets might have done. He wears dark turtlenecks all the time now." She smiled the smile of an assassin who's just had the pleasure of eliminating a professional rival.

The food truly was excellent, and we talked about that for a while. The bottle was soon empty. She asked if we should order another. I said, "Let's get just a half, shall we?" She agreed.

"So what news do you have to tell *me*?"

I said I hadn't any, that I didn't see many [that is, any] of our common friends any more.

"You certainly know one of them, and I want *all* the details, please."

I must have looked as though I had no idea what she was talking about, because of course I did not. "Oh, please. Cynthia. I heard the news and didn't believe it at first. You know how secretive she is. She wouldn't tell me a thing. I've had to go begging for scraps."

"Cynthia. I didn't know until recently that you ever knew her. You've never published with those guys."

"I saw her with you at Mulligan's that time, but I'd met her already.

She gave a talk once in Toronto to a women's group I was in. Using publicity to enhance your self-esteem. Something like that. Absolute nonsense, but she gave a good talk. We hit it off and then tried to stay in touch, as much as you can with the distance and the time difference. You must know about that."

That may or may not have been a reference to something Cynthia may have said about our LDR, I wasn't sure. In any case, I still had to ask what the news was.

"My dear, you're not keeping up. Cynthia quit her job on *ten days'* notice—they're furious with her—to move to Madrid with this Spaniard she met somewhere. You should at least try to be au courant. They left two weeks ago. She sent everyone in Canada, well, not everyone, an email saying that this is Señor Right, that she's saying farewell to Canada."

This time my shock must have been obvious to pedestrians on the pavement. I stopped breathing for a moment and I swear my heart shut down like an old generator. This time I was not certain I could hold myself together as I did at the asshole lunch in Yorkville, but I did. I remember the question I asked.

"Are you sure about this?"

"Darling, she sold or gave away everything she owned. Left with two suitcases and that's all. I was at her garage sale. You know, to show support and say goodbye—and get a look at the man, but he wasn't there, only the kids. For God's sake, I know the person who bought her car for cash."

"Kids?" This was an exclamation.

"Two boys. Beautiful Hispanic boys. Eight and twelve, I think she said."

To be merely blown away I would have needed to be restrained.

Everything came bursting out.

"My whole life has been about botched communication, but this takes the record." Eleanor looked as though she didn't get the connection. "How could she leave me without an explanation and then do this?"

"Sometimes old lovers are embarrassing, like old debts, old faux pas."

"In January I thought I was headed for grief. This is like the shock I would have had." Writing out this conversation as I remember it, which is vividly, I realise I may not have seemed to be making strict sense.

"Women are usually better at protecting themselves," Eleanor said, sensing that something was terribly wrong. "We have to be. We have to be able to close doors. Something you never quite forgive but you're sure you'll never forget—the good or the bad."

There was a few seconds' delay on her words as though a censor had his finger on the red button waiting to shut down the broadcast of anything I couldn't handle. I kept saying "How could she do this?" until I realised I was repeating myself and tried to speak more calmly. "There are things you don't know. You don't know them because they're private, but things you don't know." The gates were open now and I started to tell her the story, slowly, in an orderly manner but urgently too. "She and I were in love. Or that's what we said. But only one of us was telling the truth." Eleanor looked startled, maybe embarrassed as well, I'm not positive. I don't know how capable of embarrassment she really is. She didn't need to ask questions. I guessed what they would be and answered them for her, saying things I hadn't said aloud before.

"I know, she was at that age," I said. "The window of opportunity was closing. The clock was ticking, as they say. But she told me she really truly wanted to get pregnant and wanted me to be the father. No one's ever wanted me in that role. Then she ended it, dumped me. Never spoke to me again except to tell me to keep away from her. She changed her habits, even changed where she lived. I could have found her of course. That wasn't the point. The point is that she had evicted me from her life and refused to tell me why. I had to guess. There are scenarios that make sense. The same instinct that told her I should make the baby with her told her to leave me when I got cancer. 'Nothing personal but get out of my sight. You won't be around to be a father and a parent. You'll cheat life by dying on me and then I'll be stuck.' That's what she thought. Or I've had many long bad nights when I thought that's what she thought. Whatever combination of factors it was—being a Jew and not a rich one, being so much older, too old to coach the hockey team even if I were a Protestant sporting dad. I know this is what my father thinks. We've never gone into the details of all this. He's my father after all. But he knows what happened of course and I know how his mind works. He wasn't so much worried that his grandchildren wouldn't be Jews, because he knew that the Canadians wouldn't be able to shut them out, they would have to accept them. I guess I'm like him. Still filled with the rage sometimes. Controlling the need to control in a world that can't find a place for people like him. And I can see myself becoming like him. The difference is that he knew he wasn't the last generation. I am."

This must have been quite a performance, for I went on a bit longer about how Cynthia's last chance was likewise mine as well and that that failure is all we share now, though she will have a kind of proxy family to compensate her. I remember going on about this pandemic of botched communication ruining everything for everyone.

Eleanor was listening to all this, quite patiently as I look back now, with absolute astonishment smeared all over her face. I had never seen her so concerned, or so sincere-looking, I might add. She let me prattle on, even when I said, "You know, I should have been flattered when you called me an asshole. That's not a term for an outsider. It's something you would call an equal when you're drunk."

She looked as though she didn't follow the reasoning. I backspaced and rephrased. "Wanting to fit in is like having wanted to be part of her life. An outsider in one had to be an outsider in the other, a problem down the road. First sick, then dead, but leaving a legacy of outsiderliness. She got to the part where she knew she couldn't accept me deeply for whatever combination of reasons—health and other things. She could only accept me superficially when it was convenient. That's the way people are. Could I help their stupid little careers? 'Will you do that thing you do with my clit, you know the one?' But I've still never figured out why she's so angry. What's her equivalent of Jewish parents, immigrant exclusion, and so on? It wasn't just that she was frightened of the idea of having a child. It was more than that. I'm sure she and José will be calamitously happy."

I had talked myself into emotional exhaustion. There was a mammoth silence. Eleanor looked me in the eyes. "My God, you really don't know, do you?"

My face must have asked "Know what?"

"Jesus, I shouldn't be the one telling you this," she said.

I was collected now but growing concerned. "Go on, please. It's important."

"She was pregnant and she—dealt with it. Good Lord, you really didn't know, you poor stupid bastard?"

I didn't respond except to say to myself she had an abortion, our baby, what was going to be our baby. Even now I'm surprised that when I could get words out, they sounded so impossibly timid. "What was she thinking?"

Eleanor actually seemed to lean over the table when she said, "Not thinking maybe, but wondering."

"You mean whose it was? She was seeing other men?"

"Well, at least one apparently." She read my expression. "I don't know who." She tried to be witty at the last moment, having used up her reservoir of being supportive. "Don't you think a bitch like me would tell you if I knew?"

Questions continued to pile up in a jam inside my mouth. Why didn't she use a condom with the other guy? Why couldn't she and I have raised the child anyway? It wouldn't have been quite the same, but... It's not that the words trailed off inside my head. It's rather that the tape of memory ran out and the free end started making that terrible slapping sound.

I remember going home thinking, "I didn't know women, middle-class urban Protestant Canadian women, *did* that any longer. Wasn't that the whole point of everything that had happened since the 1970s anger against secret abortion melodramas?" I instantly thought of *Georgy Girl*, another of the English films of the sixties. Charlotte Rampling is young and attractive and gets pregnant and has a discreet abortion and then goes back to her free-spirited life. No, that's not it. She was going to have the abortion but instead she *has* the child and leaves it to be raised by Lynn Redgrave, her friend the podgy wallflower. The point is that I was actually *in* a sixties film, which is much more gripping than merely watching them thirty-some years too late. Madrid! That's absurd. She doesn't speak a word of the language and Europe is completely foreign to her in every way. This is a woman who refers to Central London as Downtown London. And he's presumably a Catholic. She probably doesn't know any more about Christianity than she does about Judaism. She likely thinks Augustine of Hippo was the Marx Brother no one talked about. No, that can't be, I don't believe she knows who the Marx Brothers were either.

Only later, in time, did I understand more. I understood that while one can have a useful relationship with an alcoholic or an addict once one learns to tap into their cycles or at least recognise a binge coming on, one can never have a relationship with someone who is impervious to subtlety and offended by candour. I understand now that the meaning of different values could also include different cities, for a person can know only one city deeply in the course of a lifetime and if he leaves it and then returns he finds it has changed beyond recognition, because cities go on forever, they are chronic until civilisation itself ends, and when you learn this lesson you are left only with the sight of new snowfall obliterating all trace of your footsteps.

ROMEO MUSIC

The only occasion in a long life when I was offered the meat of rhinoceros, I refused to eat it: a story your grandmother never tired of telling. When the war came to our section of the country, the shortage of food and other necessities became quite acute. It was not long before crowds stormed the zoo located in the park in the centre of the city and liberated the animals. Some, they say, were slaughtered on the spot, and that which the animal-killers could not carry off themselves they left for the others to pick over, particularly the women who had no men to help them. Curiously I have no memory of something so dramatic, which a person would expect even one so small to remember. Mother related the story in such a way as to suggest that by my refusal to participate in her windfall I was adding to the hardships of war. I am certain that if in fact this incident took place I was too frightened to do more than cry.

It is not simply that she was disposed towards dramatizing the past when she spoke but that the past for me has a quality that sets it apart from both the history that can be proved and the present we inhabit. Even after all these years I will still sometimes dream about the old country and the dreams are always in black and white. History is in black and white. When I departed, I left to grow and in doing so left history behind me. It startles me even now when I look in the mirror and see myself older than last month or a year ago (the pace continues to accelerate); it startles me because the entire span of my residence here has been lived in the present tense. How can the past accumulate so, how can the present become the past when I have remained so still for such a long time?

I do not know what I thought of Canada when I was a child if in fact I ever thought of Canada at all. I imagine it meant not a north-west passage but the opposite of Europe, wild Indians perhaps. When I arrived I did not expect Indians yet was still surprised by their absence. Everywhere one looked there was Ottawa and Oshawa and Mississauga, Algonquin and Algoma and Penetanguishene. It seemed an endless litany of names not English yet identical in their separate-ness. Still there were no signs of any Indians themselves, as though the effort of cataloguing it all had weakened them for some plague that followed. Not until I became a taxi driver did I get to know Indians as the taxi drivers who are paid to know such matters do. In time the questions grew more complex as my past receded and Canada loomed forever larger. The more complex the questions, the more complex the answers were. I date my attainment of a certain understanding of the unfathomable from this: the day I noticed that Nova Scotia, in French, is Nouvelle-Écosse, as though the French so hate the English that they refuse to share Latin with them but must rename what is already harmlessly foreign. But then is the foreign ever harmless if we know it is out there? Such is the way I have learned to consider things.

If we try we can imagine what it is like to be without sight. To be without sight in an unfamiliar landscape could not be so much worse. The new would grow comfortable a bit at a time; there would be a limitless supply of fresh discoveries, little private landmarks in the making. But Jesu Christi! to be mute as I was in those years, that was another matter again. Not knowing the language teaches you how to distinguish your friends and teaches you additionally how few they are.

For the first while I lived in fear of immigration detectives and worked at whatever jobs I could find and when not so working hid in whatever room I was renting. The jobs were trivial and demeaning; for the appearance of the rooms I suppose I had myself to blame. From time to time I would meet a fellow countryman. We would approach each other warily and behave like two dogs, each attempting to secure the better sniffing position before settling down to further ritual. Usually this consisted of talking in great detail about how we knew none of the same people at home. Usually we had never been to the other person's city. Differences that would have divided us back there nonetheless gave us a certain bond, which in turn caused us unease by helping break down the very distinctiveness we sought. In that place we would have been individuals. Here we were two funny men from Europe. Such certainly was my first experience of Lazlo.

Initially it was a relief to speak my own language to someone who replied in kind, but sitting in the café I would read the discomfort in Lazlo's voice as he conversed with me. In time I too began feeling as he felt. Relief became tension; repose, alertness to danger. If English people overheard us they would think we could not speak English, which Lazlo in fact was learning to do quite well. So when two country-men met we would help each other when to do so did not remind others we were foreign.

One such evening, after he had completed working for the day, Lazlo took me with him to a newspaper office situated far out in the west end of the city in a big dreary house in a street of such houses, all of which looked beaten down despite the fact they had big gardens in front. The newspaper was called the *Expository Patriot*—that is as close as translation can come to its name—and was located in the basement. Four or five other men were there as they were every night, some seated talking, others standing but hunched over under the low ceiling delineated by pipes. Lazlo introduced me.

"Stefan, this is Romano Musik, a countryman, from the south. Romano, this is Stefan about whom I have spoken, the proprietor of our newspaper."

"Musik, you are welcome here." He was grasping my hand feelingly. "You are newly arrived? So you bring news of your district and it is a burden that you have no one to tell it to." There was a tray of coffee there, and I would go back to the house several other times, many times, in succeeding weeks, and always this Stefan would first ask some question and then before hearing the answer make assumptions based upon it.

It was through Lazlo, who I sensed knew many important and unimportant people, that I got my first true job, which appeared at precisely the right moment.

I remember once that another acquaintance of this period, Yvon, one of the men with whom I fell into friendship in the evenings at the newspaper office, told me that he had come to Canada by way of New York a few years earlier and that he had for a time there made his living as a donor of blood. He would call upon a hospital to sell one or two units. Then, contrary to the regulations and common sense, he would trudge through snow to sell more at some other hospital, and so on, in a mad unsteady pattern across the city until finally, inevitably, he collapsed and became a patient of a hospital where he had previously been a patron.

At one point I was almost mad with fear—fear of being sent back if the government discovered I was not employed—and crazed with fear of hunger, the emptiness of the purse that translated not only as emptiness of the belly but as a terrible hollow feeling throughout the body, as though, if plucked with a thumb and index finger, the torso would respond with a metallic echo, a *ping*, like an old boiler, empty, useless. I shall never forget my feeling on being informed that in Canada the hospitals are forbidden to pay people for their blood.

I was more than happy when Lazlo helped me just as my money was nearly exhausted. I joined a construction crew headed by a Greek called Tolos whom Lazlo seemed to know somehow and who had eleven men working for him at different times, not always the same ones. My first day I unloaded an entire shipment of concrete blocks, slowly dismantling the thick square wall of them on the bed of the truck and creating its exact replica on the ground. I could see the blood rampaging through my veins; at night, in my room, my body ached as though I had been beaten by the police.

I held the job nearly two years and to this day I see buildings on which I worked. I date the end of my maturity from one day rounding a corner and watching a building I had helped build being torn down.

Most of the people employed by Tolos had been here much longer than I had been (some in fact were born in this country), and there was a complicated hierarchy based on who had been in Canada longer. It was a terrible sight to witness this abandonment of brotherhood in the selfish name of survival, like watching people in a lifeboat turn their thoughts towards cannibalism. I was the newest and most despised and condescended to. I was shocked when it was a country-man, Karel, a large, rough man with a face like an unleavened loaf, who chastised me the most cruelly. We were digging a trench (we preferred this to saying we were digging a ditch) and Tolos gave the signal that we were to end our labours for lunch. It was a June day but hot, like August, and the sweat was running down my face and body. My hair (I had thick black hair in those days, thicker and blacker than your own) was tangled with the heat and perspiration. I put down my tool, withdrew a comb and began forcing the hair up, out of my eyes.

"Our own Romeo," said Karel, in English. This was followed by a cooing sound. "The lover." I smiled with what I imagined was a transparent display of good nature. Those who understood no English or did not know the reference had the barb explained to them in a variety of other languages. Thereafter Karel continued to call me Romeo and others used it also until it eclipsed my true name down unto this day. Yet in time I understood perfectly well their motives, even if I still could not quite forgive him, and have long since grown used to being branded in this new country with a new name to go with it.

I could comprehend the methods and the needs of such people. In fact the longer I lived in Canada the greater the temptation to make others endlessly aware of how long I had done so. Did I hide out in the long shadow of the old homeland? I did not, at least not publicly. Yet I did not discard the old ways to the extent that I believed I did, or would like to have done, though I consciously tried to become Canadian and tried so hard that in time it began actually to happen to me. It was like a transfusion of the blood, slowly, slowly, the new displacing the old. There is no shock, no sudden unseasonable warmness of the body, just an awareness of something pleasant and beneficial. It is somewhat like what you experience at the dentist's once the needle to the gums has been withdrawn and the drug begins its work. Then there is the rude awakening when the pain later reasserts itself.

My first years, I am speaking of the period before I drove the taxi and ran the restaurant and later got my own business, my first years I would continue to haunt the newspaper office, which moved several times. Through the proprietor Stefan I met more than one important politician (I do not wish to give their names here; that is not my purpose). I became active in the Liberal riding association where I came to know several lawyers and such people. I carefully tallied my acquaintances in the Canadian community like a miser calculating the interest accruing in the bank. It was then that I changed the spelling of our name. I know you have wondered about this and so I shall explain. I felt at the time that going from Musik to Music was a graduation, also a concession to the bigger society, a harmless compromise but more importantly a possible means of making myself less foreign, though I never would have admitted that I thought with such cunning. For a time, I do not remember how long, I in fact used both spellings interchangeably, until, as old acquaintances dropped away and new growth replaced them, I was Romeo Music to one and all.

Through the same sort of natural process I found myself the business manager of the *Expository Patriot*, which meant selling advertisements and subscriptions in my evenings. Later, Stefan departed to begin a rival paper, at which time I learned that Lazlo was the true owner. He all but gave the paper to me as he withdrew into other pursuits, about which I did not inquire too closely. I was in charge and thus one day was visited by one of my Canadian political friends. A general election was to be held and he desired, so he said, my support in bringing his message to his hoped-for constituents, my readers (such as they were). The way he phrased it was to say that he wished to hear my views. I became involved with the campaign and mistook my friend's interest for patronage of me, even approval of me. Whatever it was that existed between us I used advantageously, whether he realised it or not, for I began to observe his style of dress and speech, though I still had more difficulty with English than did many of my contemporaries from the homeland.

I suppose I must put this down to some weakness but perhaps also a need for the armour that such ignorance provided (and trapped me within). There were times when I could only look to heaven in frustration at how complicated a language it is, how subtle too, to be emitted by such an unsubtle people. I date my attainment of a certain plateau from the point at which I discovered the difference between evening-dress and night-dress. Alas, by the time I learned the distinction both garments were, I am told, obsolete.[*]

I now come to the part of my life about which I have the most memories and the least to say. I know you are curious about your mother. We first met when she was helping manage the political campaign about which I have spoken, and she seemed to me untouchable. Only slowly did it occur to me that she was pressing me for more and more information about the *Expository Patriot*'s audience than could ever possibly be of any consequence to the fortunes of her friend and leader. Slowly her questioning, her apparent thirst for statistics and facts, turned to questioning of me as a man and person. As I reflect on it now ours seems to have been a most unequal relationship, if only because my desire to learn from her was genuine, hers in regard to me, not. I had answers and she only questions and a shining example.

There was, at the time of which I am speaking now, a low café on Keele Street full of bad food and music from machines on the wall.

[*] Father was apparently writing in the mid-1970s and was confused by the behaviour he saw on TV and in his own then-teenaged daughters. NM

We would meet there because it was near the constituency office. Little patches of our conversation I will remember always, though they sound inappropriate to my purpose here, uprooted from their rightful time and place, which is what history does to things. I shall not quote them except to say that your mother, I knew, cared for me without understanding me in the least and this set her apart from her many friends who neither liked nor cared. Your mother could not quite accommodate herself to the fact that I could never go back to the home country without facing certain arrest, perhaps even death.

"You mean you wouldn't even take a holiday there, to see your old friends and family?" I remember her once saying, in one of the early discussions that lasted nearly all night. I could only answer patiently but with, I suppose, the wrong tone in my voice. More than once in later years would she say I was acting in a paranoid fashion. Suffice it to say that as our relationship became more intense it provided greater opportunity for misunderstanding. Our closeness showed how far apart we were. The obvious distance illustrated the problems that our passion, we believed, could overcome.

Her friends brought out the worst in her and I the worst in her friends. In time I came to divide all people I met into categories, according to how they reacted to me. The largest category held those who thought me stupid because I could not speak the language as well as they, though as you can see I am not stupid in translation. Logic told me I should be grateful when they corrected my errors as they sometimes did, but in time this came to irritate me greatly. More irritating still was when they would supply missing words and, worst of all, speak more slowly and more loudly and explain the obvious. We were with a couple who had become our friends. Idle conversation about the things of the moment. It was towards the Christmas season and I asked the wife their plans for the holiday. She said they would visit with her husband's family in Calgary. A second elapsed and to my everlasting shock she added "Alberta," presenting the word in all its three syllables. If this sounds an unusual recollection to include here I assure you I do so only because it has seldom left my memory for long and has influenced me for many years now.

Observing my manner, you see, people would mistake it for my personality. I was automatically someone apart and always would it be so. I found myself in grotesque imaginary situations. If there were ever a war between the old country and Canada, I would be interned; if there were ever a war between the old country and Canada's enemies, I would not be listened to because I would be partisan; if ever there were a civil war in the old country, I would be left out—perhaps that was worst of all. Yet I would forever be the combination I was. I confess to you now that part of my desire to be a father was the understanding that you should be rooted here in a way no one would question, even though this meant inevitably that, even had there been no divorce, you still would have grown up without me. It meant inevitably that in nearly every important way you would become as fundamentally different from me as I am different—I see this now as my past slips farther away—from the others like you.

There is no statute of limitations. My best hope is only that when you see this after I am gone you will perhaps misunderstand me less and think of me, if you have occasion to remember, with more fondness, for after all I am your father and helped to give you life and gave you your name.

ISLANDS CRUISER

Theresa, who had beautifully thick black hair and appeared to be in her late twenties, was the second to arrive on Granville Island with her rucksack and sleeping bag. I was there already. We had never met before and neither of us had ever seen Craig, the third member of the cruising course, though when I saw him I felt as though I had because he reminded me a little of my ex. He was all muscle going to seed and blond hair not just thinning but falling out, with a tendency to project his voice way too much when he thought he was explaining something. The staff told us to wait over there in the corner, by the cardboard cartons of groceries with the name of our boat, *Islands Cruiser*, written on them. We waited for the charter skipper to arrive and herd us aboard. Then we waited some more.

Back in the nineties, as he would tell us over dinner that night, Drexler had taken the buy-out at fifty-five. He didn't know he was a cultural stereotype branded with the imprint of a particular decade, like the Vietnam War vet who can't readjust to society in all those seventies movies that guys like. There was something ridiculous about Drexler. He was shaped like one of those old bean-bag chairs and smiled at all the wrong times, exposing grey teeth. He talked a lot about his days in the Canadian Naval Reserve but had a fantasy life of being an old sea captain. After all of us carried the groceries aboard *Islands Cruiser*, a Cat 34 barely distinguishable from all the rest, like a red car in a big parking lot, he began his orientation lecture by saying how important it was that we obey all his orders instantly. "This isn't for show, it's for safety," he said. "I'm the skipper, you're crew, and inexperienced crew at that. When we're out in the middle of the Strait with the wind howling and maybe some rough seas there's no time for me to explain an order. Just do it. If you didn't understand, I'll explain it later—when there's time. Got it?" In a little while he said: "You can call me John or Skipper but I'd prefer you call me Master. This is simply the ancient nautical term, because I'm the master of the vessel." This was the most embarrassing thing he said the whole time. "Yes, Master," we all said in ragged unison. The clearest voice was Theresa's. Her lovely Asian face (she was the only Asian Theresa I'd ever heard of) betrayed not even the smallest suggestion that she read anything into having this old white man insist on her calling him her master. She was twenty-eight, I learned later, already past any anger. Either that or she was a very talented actor. All the same, I was humiliated on her behalf, on behalf of all of us in fact.

Our first night aboard we spent getting to know the boat. It was bigger than anything that any of the three of us had ever crewed on, which is why each of us had decided not to go bare boat but to pay our share of the $175 a day to get a skipper who would train us. A nice well-designed boat, handles well, but I prefer the Hunter. Drexler got angry when I said this. As it turns out, he owns *Islands Cruiser* and consigned it—and himself—to the charter fleet to help pay the bills.

"The Hunter handles like a drunk staggering up an alley," he said. "Of course, it's a matter of what you're used to, I suppose."

The Master kept the big cabin forward for himself. Craig took the bunk made by unscrewing the dining table amidships and forcing it down to form part of a sleeping surface. Theresa and I shared the aft cabin, a narrow, slightly curved space on starboard, opposite the head (this was convenient). She and I stretched out head to toe, talking a lot before falling asleep and then again each morning between waking and actually getting up, to perform our first job, making coffee. She was in the third year of her residency at a hospital in Nanaimo, but was a year behind the other people her age because she'd taken time off midway through to do volunteer doctoring in West Africa. "Family practice is where I want to be," she said. "Even after paying off my student loans." This last with a good-natured laugh. "In family practice you tend to grow old with your patients, if everybody's lucky. You watch yourself decline as they're declining. You're part of a little community with your patients. Sure some will die—you may die, in fact—but it's not like Sierra Leone. People were killed in the fighting every day, people died of AIDS every day. I'd see patients for the first time and know they wouldn't be alive when I saw them the next day, and they weren't. All the while the local physicians in the clinic were making these judgments based on tribal stuff. 'Well, she's from the such-and-such tribe. They are not a very bright tribe, you know.'"

One person cooked in the galley with its gimballed butane stove while the other two sailed, one at the helm, the other working the lines and the Master yakking endlessly when he wasn't consulting the chart and the tide tables and monitoring One Six on the marine band, all tasks he could do sitting down at his little chart table, which was near where he kept the liquor. When I was cooking, he'd occasionally come over to chip a piece of ice out of the block in the cooler. "Same damn stuff that sank the *Titanic*," he'd say, smiling at his wit. I'm pretty sure all this was strictly against the law—being drunk when the vessel was underway, I mean, not his wit, though if I'd had my way that would have been illegal too. He was deeply concerned about the possibility of any damage to *Islands Cruiser*, though in fact the boat wasn't being cared for in that obsessive-compulsive yachtsman's way. Both the standing rigging and the running rigging seemed okay, but none of the wooden rails, for instance, had been sanded and varnished in years and all the plastic panes in the windows and hatches were so heavily scratched by hail and foreign objects of one kind or another that it was almost literally impossible to see out of them. Yet the Master was fanatical about non-essentials. He'd speak sharply to me (and actually yelled at Theresa) if the detergent or the paper towels were not where he preferred them to be kept. Finally it dawned on me that this was his live-aboard, which he chartered out reluctantly whenever he needed the extra income, which was probably most of the time.

The VHF had forecast winds light to moderate across the Strait. This turned out to be irresponsibly optimistic. Tacking constantly all the way, with a steady rhythm of the boom swinging side to side, we finally reached Gabriola in seven and a half hours and came alongside at the Silva Bay marina. Even after only one day—one long, tiring day, I admit—the sexism had me pretty frustrated, and the meanness. The Master said the last time he let a charter group take out *Islands Cruiser* without him, the people returned it in dreadful condition, with the cabin full of garbage and the diesel tanks almost empty. "I put them all on the official blacklist. They will never rent a boat in this country again. If I'm lucky, they'll never be able to rent one in the

States either, at least not on the West Coast."

Theresa put up with all the nonsense beautifully. Maybe it was a function of being twenty-eight or maybe it was just the way she was and would always be, but it made the Master feel important without pandering to his idiocy. She even let Craig (an accountant with three kids) flirt with her without either flirting back or putting him off. Was she working at bonding with me? I don't think so, not unless she really *is* the best actor ever born; our relationship was quite natural. That night we were whispering in the cabin about the others. Pretending she was the Master, she drew a strand of her long hair against her top lip to make a Hitler moustache for just a minute. We laughed the whole time but kept it down.

This was in August. So when by about noon the next day there was still little wind, we persuaded the Master that we should heave-to and go for a swim. Craig just stripped to his white underpants and dived off first. He was our guinea pig. Theresa, wearing a bright red one-piece, said she saw no symptoms of hypothermia in Craig and so followed off the stern in a high arc, perfectly, exactly the way you're supposed to, like a Swiss Army knife, folding up and then unfolding again. I was in my swimsuit but too shy to get wet in it. I stayed aboard with the Master, watching Craig do antics such as going underwater and suddenly breaking the still surface in some unexpected spot far away with one of those quizzical where-am-I expressions like a harbour seal. Theresa swam completely round the boat four or five times, going from breaststroke to sidestroke to backstroke, and sometimes swimming underwater, emerging with a perfect smile and her hair flowing behind her like a cape. "Jellyfish," she called out to us from a point off the port side. Then later: "There's a cold patch over here." She was like a child who didn't want to come in from play. When she did finally climb up the hinged ladder we'd let down, her nipples were straining the top of her suit.

How can I get out of here? I began to think of jumping ship. At the end of a very long day, five-thirty in the morning to almost dark, we put into Clam Bay with the Master full of whisky sours, shouting commands. We dropped the Bruce anchor from the bow, gently played out perhaps fifty feet of rode and put the throttle in reverse, slowly, carefully, until we could all feel what I imagine the last cinch in a Victorian corset must have felt like. Except for our leader, we were a good team.

Maybe a dozen other vessels, mostly other sailboats but a couple of powerboats as well, were at anchor too. There was enough light left to see that there was nothing much at Clam Bay except a couple of small sheds, part of the reserve, but no moorage of any kind and no store, not even anything you could call a beach. Darkness fell like a dropped shoe and I couldn't any longer make out the silhouette of the Master holding his glass, but his voice carried over the water. The white anchor lights at the tops of all the masts mimicked the unobstructed stars. The Master had left the dingy out. As I lay in my bunk, inches from Theresa, I thought of sneaking up the companionway, untying the painter, and slipping away to shore in the blackness. It was only forty metres or so. But how would I get my gear together without turning on the light or row ashore without being detected? In any case, there was no way out of Clam Bay. No ferry from anywhere to anywhere else, no boats to hire. Besides, the old bastard would probably have had me charged with theft. No, with piracy. He'd like the sound of that.

Our destination was Snug Cove on Bowen Island but on the way we had to put in at Chemainus for ice, as the food was going off pretty quickly. The way our Lord and Master kept raiding the ice-box for his drinks, rather than for snacks like the rest of us did, hadn't helped. BC Ferries stopped here of course. Even an internet café had opened up since I was last there, and the trend towards cuteness and antique shops with imported antiques and locally made fudge had increased. I now had my bag secretly packed and could have got off, but there were problems. I was never alone. We all went to the grocery as a group. We went everywhere as a group, except when the M made a solitary call at the government liquor store. Besides, as much as I wanted to get away from him, I wanted just as much not to be away from T. A quick goodbye and farewell seemed the best plan.

We finally had a little bit of wind going across the Strait enroute to Snug Cove. Not much but enough to get some speed. The M stood up in the cockpit, holding onto the rod running through the dodger, saying, "My God, can't you feel the adrenalin?" The rest of us looked at one another as if to say: "No, actually." We came alongside at the Union Steamship pier. Bowen has always seemed to me to suffer the same relationship to Vancouver that Marin County does to San Francisco. It must have been a nice place once when it was under-populated, maybe in the fifties or sixties, I'm not sure when. Now it's packed with former hippies who've grown rich and go to bed every night worrying that their pubic hair is turning grey. They compensate by honking the horns on their SUVs in the morning rush hour as they board the ferry for the short shuttle to Horseshoe Bay and ultimately downtown, with its big banks (none as big as the mountains, though, not yet) and maze of other mazes.

I found myself alone for a moment, plugging into shore power and doing other little chores while T, C and the M hurried off ashore for their various reasons, to make phone calls, take showers, and such.

This was my chance. With them out of sight, I got my gear as quickly as I could and hopped ashore. Then I thought about getting a room for the night, just to decompress in. A decompression chamber. The rooms at the marina were booked up, so I tried a couple of B&Bs, without success. I went to the tourist office next to the barbershop to get a list of them all (there must be scores, advertised and otherwise) but the building was closed. I was reading the schedule to find out the time of the next ferry when Craig came by with a surprised look on his face after seeing my sleeping bag and other stuff. "I'm jumping ship," I said. "Going to be a castaway." I fixed my eyes on the timetable again so that he'd pass by with only a smile, which he did. Less than a minute later, I'd just turned round to haul my stuff to the ferry dock when I saw the Master come up to me arrogantly, carrying a case of beer on one of his round shoulders.

"Where do you think you're going?" He launched into a short, sharp, and totally one-sided argument, saying finally, "Well, do whatever the fuck you want, bitch."

I shouted after him, "Have a good trip home." But he pointedly didn't answer.

From the top deck of the ferry a half-hour later I could see him and Craig sitting in the cockpit of *Islands Cruiser* drinking beer. I strained but couldn't see Theresa. I suspect she was below, making dinner for the boys. I never saw her again. I wish I were her patient. I'd trust her with my life.

AZIZ & LEON

Leon's colleagues in Political Science thought he was a fool. He believed they were speaking to him through the papers they gave, the books they published, the societies they belonged to, and the conferences they attended: the way a demented person in the Downtown Eastside might believe that CSIS or the American military communicates through the paper foil in cigarette packages or the beeps emitted by crosswalk signals for the benefit of the visually impaired. What Leon thought they were saying—and he was right—was Pacific Rim, Pacific Rim, Pacific Rim. That's where the funding was, that's where the future was, it's where the students were. Leon was the only person in the department, the only full professor at either university, still interested in contemporary European politics. Many considered him a throwback, but he thought he had a nice arrangement worked out, with contacts in the two Germanys and Poland and Hungary who were eager to publish and entertain him, and indeed listen to the opinions of this colleague from the West. He was their conduit. They solicited his views earnestly and translated what he wrote. His report to the dean at the end of the year always made for impressive reading. Then the bottom fell out.

The Solidarity movement in Poland, the tearing down of the Wall, reunification, and of course something he'd never dreamed he'd see, the collapse of the Soviet Union. For a while he was in considerable demand as an instant expert for the CBC and other news organizations, giving meaning to the chaos by laboriously writing a few sound bites for himself and repeating them time and again with only slight revision.

While the good times lasted, he easily might have suggested flying to Europe to soak up the hospitality of their grey and decrepit governments by crossing the Pacific, but he always chose the other way, across the Atlantic, stopping at Toronto and London to decompress. After the first time, his wife got bored and never wanted to go with him on research trips, but contented herself with summers keeping busy in North Van with the teenagers. At least it was better than having to be a faculty spouse in languages she didn't understand in places in which she had no interest. Secretly she sort of wished he had gone over to Pacific Basin Studies when the boom started in the late seventies and early eighties.

✳ ✳ ✳

Aziz's enemies enjoyed saying that back in the old country his family bought and sold goats. Or maybe these weren't his enemies but simply people who envied him, admired his initiative and sought some way to account for his success. Or to explain it all away out of jealousy. He wasn't sure. In any case, Aziz, who in fact had once studied chemistry at the university, briefly, took to business in his new homeland like a natural. If only he could have mastered English with as little effort.

When he opened his first shop, a customer came in and said "Morning." Of course it was morning, Aziz thought. Days passed before he figured out that this was a short form of Good Morning, a Canadian greeting. He then began hailing everyone who entered this way. This is how you learn. He learned most of all from the *Sun*, which began business in October 1971, the same month that he arrived. The coincidence made him feel a special kinship with the paper, as though he and its columnists were part of the same club. He read them carefully every day to improve his English, but his progress, though steady, was discouragingly slow. To engage customers in conversation he would sometimes repeat opinions he had read. Sometimes this worked, sometimes not, depending on the customer. After more than twenty years his English was good enough for him to recite from the newspaper from memory but not good enough to let him debate, defend or even explain what he was saying if challenged.

But he knew what he was reading all right, for in a way he owed his luck to the *Sun* (he was a superstitious man). He found his first premises through one of its classifieds. "Roncesvalles-Queen small retail apt above, ideal mom-and-pop. Some fixtures." He kept his faith even after good fortune deserted him and the business went belly up because he had carried too much inventory in an area that already had too many convenience stores, all of them with prices lower than his. Besides, some people complained to the city after they got sick eating frozen fish that had thawed while the old freezer was broken and then had been refrozen once it was fixed. Aziz moved to another part of the city with fewer rivals and even less floor space.

By this time he had learned to start up without spending too much. Some tricks were just little things. When a liquidator's auction was advertised in the *Sun*, he would arrive at the sale after most of the other bidders had left and the last lots were coming up. His cousin (who later proved to be a thief) would cover the store at such times. Generally there was one lot consisting of all the assorted leftovers of a once-healthy business: the cash register, maybe a glass case or two, and one large carton containing a Chargex printer, rubber stamps, office supplies and the like. Some of it could be sold to pay for the rest. One of his best tricks was attending stamp auctions. Collectors and dealers usually weren't interested in buying sheets of brand new or recent stamps. He could get them for far less than the sum of their face value, then sell them as new in the store, using one- and two-cent denominations to make up the price of first-class postage. A little extra licking. No one seemed to mind. This was business the law couldn't catch him for.

✳ ✳ ✳

Leon had a post office box, she didn't know why. He said he'd had it for years, that he'd needed it during his previous marriage and kept it for receiving printed material from countries behind the Iron Curtain that he didn't want to receive at home or at the university. Not a big thing. But the last time he was away in Berlin—Berlin had become the focus of his research, he could go on about it for hours—she called the accountant to see where their pitifully small one-time-only tax refund cheque had got to. The accountant consulted his records and found that his office had had it sent to the post office box by mistake. She had to phone Leon at the hotel in Berlin to ask where he kept the key. He sounded reluctant, but finally told her. It was hidden inside a certain book in his den. She retrieved it, went to the post office, and got the cheque, and also brought home for him whatever else was in the box. Dry political newspapers and magazines she couldn't read except to know that they were dry, and one strange-looking envelope, its whole upper-right quadrant covered in brightly coloured German stamps. The handwriting was unmistakably European but also slanty and childlike. She opened it. Out fell Polaroids of a young man sitting naked in a plain wooden chair, his head thrown back, one hand stroking an absolutely enormous erection. He looked like he was on the verge of ejaculating all over the camera, just on the cusp of transportation to some gigantic momentary ecstasy. A type of greeting or wisecrack was written in German along the wide bottom margin of this particular photo. The immature hand that had written it must be the same one that was getting exercise in the picture. (If he was a right-handed masturbator, then wouldn't he write right-handedly as well?)

Her first reaction was panic, followed quickly by a sense of being broken inside and then a little crazed. She went on a tear through the den, through the whole house, the closets. Then she drove to the campus and talked her way into his office, saying that he'd stupidly left their income tax cheque there. She ransacked the filing cabinet, the desk. She felt a small sense of guilt but that was swamped by her multiplying humiliation. Finally she discovered a kind of wooden strongbox and sat down and read with horror and disgust—disgust at deception by the father of the girls—a thick bundle of letters from someone named Dieter, who wrote in a peculiar English indeed but who was easy enough to understand when he wished to be, particularly in the parts about wanting to fuck Leon in the ass again. Many contained photos, some Polaroids, others real prints. Some showed Dieter's face. He looked about twenty or so. Leon kept copies of his own letters, so that, when she returned to North Van, her heart hammering as she waited impatiently to get across the damn bridge, she began to arrange the correspondence in chronological order according to the postmark or date on the first page until there were only a few gaps in the whole story. They wrote as though each was practising the other's language but also used the secret language of lovers. The affair seemed to have been going on since before Dieter had even been legally an adult. All those academic papers, all those conferences on European security.

✳ ✳ ✳

As a *Sun* reader, Aziz worshipped the police and the authorities on principle, but in practice he hated the fact that there were as many laws here as there were in the old country and that, here as there, he had to obey them or work hard to avoid them. The law kept him from selling cigarettes to kids though cigarettes had the fastest turnover and the highest margin of any category of goods not actually stolen: no one would ever accuse him of selling cigarettes that were stale. One night after he closed, some kids smashed his window to steal junk radios and a plastic CN Tower with a clock and a thermometer in it (CN Tower collectibles were starting to be big by then). He didn't have insurance to cover the cost of the broken glass. In the old country, his brothers and his various cousins would have found the kids and beaten them. The law made him keep dirty magazines on the top row, high enough off the floor so that kids couldn't reach them, though these too were very profitable. The dirty-magazine bylaw made him angry sometimes. Columnists in the *Sun* vented anger about other things but through anger they made him feel that they were giving voice to rage that he himself wasn't articulate enough to express, at least not in good English. Himself, he didn't read the dirty magazines;

they didn't sell well if soiled. Eventually, though, he discovered the *Northern Miner*, which he would turn to when business was slow and he was finished with the day's *Sun*. Doing so, he dreamed a dream he had dreamed many times back home, of going to the North, where there weren't so many laws, and prospecting for gold or silver, maybe both. Geology was not so far removed from chemistry after all. If he struck it rich, he would return to the old country a rich Canadian.

That was at about the time that the first provincial lotteries began. He quickly saw some potential to get rich peddling the same dream to other people. The province sold you the tickets at a discount and took back the unsold ones over the following week or month. They brought in at least as much money as cigarettes and, in time, even more—at moments of peak public greed, almost as much as cigarettes and dirty magazines combined. When the first scratch-and-wins came in, customers would buy one when they brought their other purchases to the counter. They would use a coin or a dirty fingernail to scrape away the black strip (like the ones over people's eyes in old pornographic pictures) to see if they had a winner underneath. Sometimes they won five dollars or even ten. Most of the time they won nothing and let the useless paper fall to the floor. Aziz started to gather up the old tickets when he swept out the place every night immediately before closing.

✳ ✳ ✳

During that winter Aziz began experimenting late into the small hours with creating a coating that would reconceal the number. His first attempts were clumsy and looked nothing like the original and either came off with the slightest friction or else proved totally indelible. Finally, after labouring like a mad bomber hating the law so much that he worked away in a secret makeshift laboratory in the cellar, he came up with an ink that looked quite convincing, not bad at all. In order to have enough tickets that he could hide a bogus one among the returns, he had to tell customers that he was already sold out that week. He slipped one of his revitalized tickets into a batch of unused ones he was returning. And nothing happened. Emboldened, he kept at it, but now he was rubbing off the tickets' original emulsion to see if he had struck it rich (he never did) before doctoring them to sell to people off the street. He was careful to deal mainly with persons who were too preoccupied to notice. One night, however, he slipped one to a fellow who was apparently not so drunk as he seemed.

※ ※ ※

After hiring a clever lawyer, Aziz was allowed to serve the sentence on weekends on the grounds that, since his cousin had returned to the old country in failure, he had no one to look after the shop and would become a burden on society if he were forced out of business entirely, as he had no other family or friends in Canada he could trust to keep the place open and couldn't afford an employee. The Don Jail, time after time, was terrifying, but the worst humiliation was the report of his case in the *Sun*.

As for Leon, I've run into him only a few times since the divorce, the scandal. Once, before he took early retirement, I saw him at the university gym, where he hoped to get some basic exercise instruction, no doubt for the first time in his life. They wouldn't let him on the gym floor because although he had bought a brand new track suit and a thing to keep his glasses on while working out, he was still in his black leather-soled shoes (with black socks). I didn't see him often after that but whenever I did I noticed that he was less helpless than he'd been the first time, and more angry. At whom, I'm not sure. One day I spied him walking along the street in a heavy rain without an umbrella or even a hat. He had a sour expression and his pipe was clenched tightly between what I always assumed were his false teeth. To keep the rain out of the bowl, he had turned the pipe upside down. He hurried along but without undue haste, getting wetter and wetter, pointedly ignoring the panhandlers except to glare at them with a brief but frightening insight.

THE OXFORD BOOK OF EVERYDAY LIFE (EXCERPTS)

We decided we were going to get married at City Hall and were going to write our own vows. I wanted us to do it together but he kept changing the subject and so I finally figured that we had better each write our own. It was hard. I'd try to show him what I'd written and get some input but he'd only look at it for a second or two and I couldn't get any response out of him. At the wedding, when they told us to go ahead and read what we'd prepared, he went first, and I couldn't believe it. He was stealing my vows and using them as his own! I could have killed him then and there—a widow at my own wedding, that would have been a first. I don't think I ever forgave him.

She had that look you always recognize even if you've never seen it before. Her arms were so thin they were like reinforcing rods. Her eyes reminded me of the eyes that taxidermists use. We sang "Happy birthday to you, happy birthday to you, happy birthday dear Grandma, happy birthday to you." She couldn't blow out even one candle. Three weeks later she died of emphysema. We always thought the cancer would get her first, but we were wrong.

I always say if you live long enough Eddie Fisher will make a comeback. The other day on the radio they had a mystery singer and I knew right away 'cause the clue was that he was from Toronto. You probably don't remember him. Bobby Breen. He was a young kid, maybe thirteen or fourteen, and was on the Eddie Cantor show on TV and won a trip to Hollywood. He was from right down at Bathurst and Dundas. His voice changed and his career fell apart.

At one point we were so close I could hear the police radios squawking like parrots.

She: When I was pregnant the first time and almost died, he seemed to blame me for everything, as though I was threatening him with even more responsibility than he had to begin with. He did everything he could to avoid me. Worked around the clock. He: Sometimes I could swing it to work two shifts. So I joined a gym a couple blocks from the garage and I'd work out for a couple hours in between. I never figured out how much overtime I needed to pay for the gym. Needing money made me tense. Spending it just so I could work out made me tense too.

He must have decided all of a sudden. The cops say he left a wake-up call.

It used to be that all the roads seemed to feed into the city, the way all the streams feed into rivers and all the rivers feed into the lake and then, I guess, the ocean. I remember once, twenty-five years ago, spotting him one day in the middle of the afternoon, walking backwards on the railway track, with a case of twelve and singing to himself. That's why I was surprised to see him crying in the subway and calling everybody a son of a bitch when they wouldn't give him any money. I couldn't believe it was the same person. Of course, if he'd recognized me, maybe he would have felt the same. It's not the kind of thing we say about ourselves, though, is it?

After his wife died he had to look after himself. One day he took a suit to the cleaners and forgot to take his Order of Canada out of the lapel. He never got it back of course. After that he was never really the same. Most of the time he stayed home and read detective novels, one after another. Sometimes he'd realize about page fifty it was one he'd read before. As time wore on, it would be page one hundred or one-fifty before he noticed. True story. 'Course what he'd forgotten, and what the people who had to take care of him never knew anything about, is that you just buy another of the damn pins from a place in Toronto. They don't sell them out here. You've got to order from back east.

I only took up smoking again to get rid of the four pounds I put on during the holidays, but now I have to give it up, no fooling around this time. This is important. Having a baby will put structure in my life and help me finish the dissertation.